ESCORTING THE PLAYER

THE ESCORT COLLECTION, BOOK ONE

LEIGH JAMES

CMG PUBLISHING, LLC

CHAPTER 1

CHASE

I was just about to head to practice when my phone buzzed.

Jessica: i won't be here L8R

im leaving u 4realz this time

I groaned. My wife, who was a *magna cum laude* graduate of Brown University, was texting me about the state of our marriage...and the texts were written in sixth-grade gibberish.

Chase: Why?

Jessica: because u r an obsessed prick

Chase: I told you I was sorry.

Jessica: whatev

Chase: Why are you texting me? Aren't you in the next room? And why no grammar?

Jessica: here 4now

grammar = NM ur 2 old u don't get it

Just fucking perfect. She was leaving me this time for "realz". As for the rest of what she'd said…I had no idea what it meant.

This was my team's first day back and I didn't have time for this. Still, I had to do damage control. If there was one thing I'd learned, it was that Jess would not be ignored. I took a deep breath and headed to the bedroom, where I found her. She was playing with her long, dark hair and inspecting what appeared to be her entire wardrobe, neatly assembled on the bed next to an open suitcase.

"What do you want?" she asked. She sounded bored.

"Just thought I'd check in," I said, leaning back against the wall and crossing my arms against my chest. "Since you're leaving me and all."

She didn't look at me. "I told you I wanted that show. Since you pulled the plug, I've just been sort of…done."

"I know you're disappointed. But the timing wasn't right, just like the timing's not right for this." I jerked my chin toward the suitcase. "Let's sit tight before we make any decisions, okay? We just need to get through this season—it's important to me and you know it."

"That show was important to me and *you* knew it. I just wanted something for myself, for once." She started filling her Louis Vuitton suitcase with thousands of dollars' worth of clothes and I struggled to feel sorry for her.

"Are you serious?" I asked. She'd threatened to leave me so many times, I'd lost count. The packing was a first, though. She'd never actually packed.

It's not like I want her to stay. It's just not a good time for her to leave. This was my season, dammit. I needed it to be perfect.

"You don't have to pretend to care," she said, carefully refolding a sweater. "If that's what you're doing."

I sighed. Maybe there wasn't ever a good time for your wife to leave you. But I was coming up on my final season as a quarterback for the New England Warriors. I had to focus on my team, not on the personal drama that was unfolding—or actually, *was* folding—in my bedroom.

"What do you want?" I asked. There had to be something. Her list of demands had kept growing—from an engagement ring, to a huge wedding, to a tricked-out Jaguar F-Pace and a ten-thousand-dollar a week spending allowance. And then the series. She'd *really* wanted the series, but I'd said no. I couldn't put myself on public display like that. It was bad for the team and for my reputation.

She was still having a temper tantrum about it.

Jess sighed. "It's too late now. And we should at least be honest with each other. We've been over for so long, we need a new word for over."

"I don't want you to do this."

She finally looked at me, her Botox-laden upper lip struggling to raise itself into a look of disdain. *She'd been so pretty when I met her.* "I'm sure you don't—it's inconvenient. But we both know it's not because you care about me. You don't care about anybody… Not even yourself."

I ran my hands over my closely cropped hair. "You're being crazy. What the hell are you even talking about?"

"I'm talking about football, Chase." She rolled her eyes. "That's the only thing you love. It's taken me this long to figure it out. Excuse me for wanting something more out of life."

Dismissing me, she went back to packing.

I numbly watched her. When I'd started dating Jessica, she'd fawned over me. She used to make me green smoothies. She used to give me massages...and hour-long blow jobs.

I'd confused that with being a nice person.

In retrospect, that was a reasonable mistake. You can think a lot of stupid things when you're getting a blowjob. But as soon as the ink was dry on our marriage license, it'd been all about Jess. No more smoothies. No more massages. She was too busy shopping and getting "refreshed" by her plastic surgeon. She only blew me when she was about to ask for something outrageously expensive. As soon as her mouth started heading for my happy trail, I knew to reach for my wallet.

She'd trained me well.

I'd been blind. A dumbass thinking with his Johnson. Being a professional athlete, I should've known better, but I'd honestly thought she loved me. Because who wouldn't, right?

This is where being a cocky son-of-a-bitch broke down.

Jessica didn't love me. She loved the limelight, the clothes, the big house. Once I figured that out, I'd put up with it because I was trying to keep things on an even keel. I needed to focus on my career. Now she was packing up her four-thousand-dollar suitcase to leave me right before the most important season of my life was about to begin.

And I just stood there, not knowing whether to laugh or cry.

~

AVERY

"Lila." I nudged my sister's sleeping form, which was sprawled out across my bed.

"Stop," she mumbled and rolled over.

"You're supposed to go to work. You have to get up."

She either pretended to not hear me or couldn't hear me, I didn't know which. She'd been out until the early hours of the morning, doing God only knew what. I looked at the clock—she needed to be in Harvard Square in twenty minutes.

"Lila. Please. Rent's due, remember?"

She pulled the covers over her head and ignored me. She was going to get fired from yet another job. This one was Jamba Juice. The last one was Starbuck's. She'd gone from getting and losing jobs in the city's high-end restaurants to getting and losing jobs in the city's chains. She was so pretty, with her long, wavy blond

6

hair and perfect skin, that she often got hired on the spot.

Then the trouble would start.

I looked at the five-foot-six, one-hundred-thirty-pound pile of trouble hiding under the blankets on my bed. Even though Lila was my older sister, I was the responsible one. I was the one who'd always taken care of her, even before our mother died. But she didn't seem to appreciate it. She treated me like a nagging, over-protective parent—except when she was trying to wheedle an allowance out of me.

I went out to the tiny kitchen and grabbed the portable safe I'd recently bought. I hated to spend the money on it, but I didn't trust my sister with cash in the house. I entered the combination and counted the money inside. One thousand dollars, courtesy of my last assignment.

Our rent was due in two days—nine-hundred ninety-five dollars.

It looked like I was going to be eating five dollars' worth of Ramen noodles—and *only* five dollars' worth of Ramen noodles—for the foreseeable future.

At least all my hooker clothes would fit.

Way to find the upside, Avery.

I bit my lip, thinking of my hooker clothes. *Escort clothes.* The madam had lent me two outfits for the assignments I'd done. One was a mini dress and thigh-high boots. The other was a filmy black dress that my tits had practically hung out of, much to the delight of the John.

I was going to have to call Elena again. I needed another assignment, fast. I didn't want to do it—not calling her, not *any* of what happened after that. But I'd made thirty dollars on my last waitressing shift. Our landlord had already started eviction proceedings against us twice. And since Lila didn't appear to be getting out of bed anytime soon, and I didn't want to start sleeping in a cardboard box on the sidewalk next month, I didn't really have a choice.

I checked the time. If I could get Lila up and throw some clothes on her, she might only be ten minutes late for her shift. Maybe it was salvageable. I hustled back to my room, throwing the door open dramatically, hoping to rouse her.

But she was already awake. She was sitting up on my bed, smoking a joint.

"Jesus Christ, Lila!" I wailed. "Put that out and go to work."

She shook her head and exhaled, causing a greasy, gray cloud of smoke to hang over my bed. "You should seriously try weed, Ave. You need to chill."

My heart sank. She just didn't get it. "I *need* to pay our rent."

She shrugged. "So go call your agency. They paid you a ton the last time."

She inhaled again and I saw ashes fall onto my bedspread. I fought back the desperate urge to smack her. Or cry. "That's really nice, Lila. You go ahead—just stay in bed with your joint. Don't you worry about getting fired from another job. I'll go sell my body for money so you can *relax*. I'll take care of everything." My voice was dripping with sarcasm, but my sister looked largely undeterred.

"Promise me you'll take care of her," my mom said. "Some people just need...help. Your sister's one of them."

My sister who was smoking a joint on my bed, about to be fired from her fifth consecutive job.

Lila exhaled and coughed a little. "Don't be so dramatic," she said. "I mean it, Ave, take a hit."

I crossed my arms against my chest. "I'm about to hit *you.*"

My sister giggled. "Don't be mean," she said, her voice turning into a whine, "I hate it when you're mean."

"Then don't force me into it." I sighed. "Seriously... can you *please* get dressed and go to work?"

Guilt flashed in her eyes. "The thing is? I don't actually *have* a shift today. Something happened with the manager, and I had to tell her to go to hell..."

I sighed, listening to Lila's latest tale of getting fired and how it wasn't her fault. But in the back of my mind, all I was thinking about was calling Elena.

I was going out on another assignment. Whether I liked it or not.

CHAPTER 2

CHASE

I drove to our first scheduled workout of the season, a dull headache throbbing as I navigated the highway. Eric, my best friend and agent, called me on the way in.

"How's my favorite client?" He sounded like he always did—as if he was cruising around Los Angeles, the sunroof to his SUV wide open, living the good life of a top talent agent.

"I've been better," I admitted. "I'm pretty sure Jessica's moving out today."

"Shut the fuck up," Eric said. "For real this time?"

I took the turn that would lead me to the enormous stadium. "Seems like it. She was packing when I left."

Eric let out a low whistle. "I don't know whether to say sorry or…yay."

"Ha ha." My headache got incrementally worse. "I don't know, either."

"Did you call Mickey yet?" Mickey was my attorney. The one who'd begged me two years ago to do a pre-nuptial agreement, an idea that Jessica had completely shot down with the aid of crocodile tears.

I laughed. "Not yet. He's gonna have a field day with this."

"He told you so," Eric said.

"You all did," I admitted.

"Even your Mom, dude. You should always listen to Martha."

I groaned. Of all the phone calls I was dreading, the one to my Mom was at the top of the list.

"She warned you."

My headache moved to between my eyes. "I know—okay? You don't need to be so sanctimonious. Last time I checked, you weren't exactly a relationship guru. It's not like your wife's perfect—oh wait, that's right, you don't *have* a wife."

"Neither do you, apparently." He started to laugh and I couldn't help it, I did, too. Then I thought about all the money Jess was going to be looking for and all of the shit she was probably going to start, and the laughter died on my lips.

"Talk to Mickey and call your Mom—not necessarily in that order," Eric ordered. "And buddy, I wouldn't tell anybody else about this if I were you. Let's see if Jess is there when you get back. If not, maybe we should think about getting out in front of this."

"Huh?" Eric was a schemer. He was usually two steps ahead of me in that department, which was why he'd made partner at a top talent agency at thirty years old.

"We should maybe leak something to the press," Eric explained matter-of-factly. "Let the story out a little bit at a time so we can control the message and the tone."

My gut twisted. This was not the sort of press I'd been hoping for this year. "Huh."

"Call Martha," Eric instructed again before hanging up.

I pulled into the parking lot at the stadium and took an Advil. It was still morning, but the day had completely gone to shit.

And it was about to get worse. I hit my mother's number. "Hey, Ma."

She clucked her tongue as soon as she answered. "Well, the world-famous quarterback remembers to call his mother for once. How's my favorite son?"

"I'm your only son," I groaned.

"Aw, honey, you're still my favorite boy. Just like your sister's still my favorite girl."

I steeled myself. "Well, your favorite son has some news."

"What's the matter?" She was quiet for a second, her mom-radar probably going into overdrive. "Is Jessica trying to get you to go to Boca Raton for the holidays again? I swear to God, Chase, if she pulls that this year—"

"She's leaving me," I interrupted.

My mother snorted. "If I had a dime for every time that ungrateful gold digger threatened to leave you... that'd be a lot of dimes, dear."

I grimaced. "She's packing, Ma. Feel free to say 'I told you so.'"

"I *did* tell you so—and that's because I'm always right. But I'm still sorry." Martha seemed to consider the news for a moment. "So, who is it?"

"Huh?"

"The guy she's leaving you for?" She sounded as though she were being patient with me.

"What?" I asked, feeling dazed. "I don't think that's what's going on—"

"Jessica's not leaving you and your piles of money and your mansion in Wellesley because she needs personal space," she said, interrupting me. "Of *course* there's someone else."

I squeezed the bottle of Advil. I would appreciate it if

my mother was wrong, for once.

"Don't you worry," Martha clucked. "No matter who it is, nobody's better than you. Anyways, good riddance to bad rubbish. I always thought that Jessica was like that Ursula from *The Little Mermaid*—she could make herself appear beautiful, but underneath it she was ugly. *Real* ugly. Like, run away screaming ugly. You remember Ursula, don't you, honey? The bad witch who was an octopus?"

"I don't know what you're talking about," I groaned. "I never saw *The Little Mermaid*—"

"Oh, of course you did," she said, sounding exasperated. "And *Cinderella*, and *Sleeping Beauty*…you watched all the princess movies with me and your sister. Remember?"

"I gotta go, Ma," I said, holding onto the ibuprofen for dear life.

AVERY

I called in to AccommoDating while I was on break at the *Sizzling Ranch*. "Hey. It's Avery Banks."

"Nice to hear from you again, Avery," Elena, the madam, said politely. "What can I do for you?"

"I need an assignment." I bit my lip.

"When are you available?"

"As soon as I'm done with my waitressing shift. I'm free tonight," I said. My stomach roiled with nerves.

"I'll see what I have coming in," Elena said smoothly. "I'd love to get you working some more. The other clients were very pleased with you."

"Thank you," I mumbled. I shoved the images of the other clients forcefully from my mind. Then I went back to work, my hands shaking.

A girl I waitressed with had told me about AccommoDating.

"My sister went to a wedding this weekend," Kylie had said, while we were cleaning the chain restaurant's equipment and readying for the day.

I'd smiled at her, trying to be friendly. "Oh yeah?"

"Uh-huh. She said it was high-class, all the way. She got flown to an *island*. In the *Caribbean*. All expenses paid. It was a bunch of billionaires or something." Kylie wiped down the soda machine and simultaneously tossed her thick, curly ponytail over her shoulder. "'Wouldn't *I* like to meet a billionaire', I told my sister. You know what she said?"

"No," I answered. I didn't know Kylie that well, but I liked her. She was always talking, always had a story to tell. I appreciated that. Her friendly chatter helped pass the long shifts at the restaurant.

Kylie moved on to the coffeemaker and wiped it almost violently. "She told me it'd never happen—that I'd never get a billionaire because I'm not pretty enough. And 'cause I talk too much."

I gave her a consoling look. "I'm sorry. It's not true—you're very pretty. It's just sister shit. I have one. She can be mean, too."

Kylie gave me a conspiratorial look. "Mine's a *hooker*," she said in a low voice. "So you'd think she wouldn't be such an uppity you-know-what, but she still is."

I was completely taken aback. "For real?" I asked, finally.

She nodded. "For real. I shouldn't say she's a hooker. She's an *escort*, is what she calls it. She gets wined and dined all the time. The wedding she just went to? One of her escort friends was the *bride*. She married a billionaire who was one of her clients."

"Wow." It was all I could think of to say.

"You should do it," Kylie said, nodding at me. "You've got the look. Perfect skin. Rocking body. All that blond hair and those big blue eyes. And you're quiet, unlike me."

I laughed, but it came out bitter and sharp. "I don't think I'm...qualified. Sexy isn't really my thing, you know?"

Kylie tossed her ponytail over her shoulder again.

"My sister got paid ten thousand dollars for one night once," she said. "I think you could fake the sexy for that."

I felt my jaw drop. "So why don't *you* do it?" I asked, wondering if she was just teasing me.

She grunted. "Maya said she'd blackball me. She said I seriously talk too much and she doesn't want to be associated with me at work. But I'm not kidding, girl. If you want the number, I'll give it to you. Maybe you'll marry a billionaire and set me up with one of his friends. Or eventually put in a good word for me at the agency."

I shook my head. "I don't think I could do it. I'm too shy. And I'm not exactly, uh, *experienced.*" I felt my face flame.

"You're a *virgin?*" Kylie's eyeballs looked as though they might pop out of her head.

"No," I said quickly. "But I've only ever had one boyfriend. And he was pretty…vanilla."

"Think about it." Kylie shrugged. "I know you're broke. I've seen you stealing crackers to eat."

My face got even hotter. I *did* steal packages of crackers; I pretended that I had to go to the bathroom and stuffed them into my mouth as often as I could. I was always hungry, shaking from the emptiness inside me. Kylie had seen me. She'd known, and she felt sorry for me.

Being poor was so fucking humiliating.

"In case you change your mind," Kylie said. She scribbled something onto a cocktail napkin and slid it into my apron. "It'd be nice to be able to eat three squares a day, right? And it's *gotta* beat waitressing."

I'd pulled out the napkin after my shift. It had the name and number of the agency.

I didn't call for a few weeks. Not until Lila got fired from her third consecutive job and had started burning through my limited supply of cash at an alarming rate. There hadn't even been enough money for Ramen.

Hunger could drive you to crazy things.

And then there was my sister, who seemed to be getting even more adrift. She was my responsibility, my family. I needed to take care of her. I hadn't been able to save my mom, but Lila was going to be another story. *If only she'd cooperate.*

So I called the service. I'd taken a couple of clients. Neither of them were that bad, but I'd still cried afterwards. It was just that I'd always tried to be a good girl. I'd tried to be a good girl my whole life, and still, I couldn't get ahead.

And it didn't seem to matter to anyone.

Except to me.

CHAPTER 3

CHASE

"Hey hey hey, there's the big guy," called Reggie, our running back and one of my closest friends on the team. He patted me on the shoulder. "You ready to work?"

"Yeah," I said. Work was the one thing I was looking forward to today. As the starting quarterback for the Boston Warriors for the past five years, I'd led us to two Super Bowl wins. At thirty-seven, this season would be my last. I had great expectations. I wanted another Super Bowl ring. I had several NFL records in my sights. But I had to stay healthy, and I had to stay smart. I couldn't let this stuff with Jessica mess with my head and ruin everything I'd worked so hard for.

I turned to my teammate. "How about you? You ready to rumble?"

He grinned at me. "Not like I got anything better to do than kick some ass."

Someone snorted behind us. Pax Unger, our new cornerback, swaggered in. "Word on the street is that you're ready to retire, Reggie," he said, his tone nasty.

"Oh man—why do you always have to start that shit?" Reggie asked.

Pax shrugged and threw his locker open. He started to change, and I noticed that he looked bigger than last year. "I'm not starting shit," Pax said, feigning innocence. "But you two are both getting old. And football's no country for old men."

"Will you shut up, for once?" I asked, throwing my practice jersey on over my pads. "If I had a dime for every time you talked shit...then I probably *could* retire."

Reggie laughed, but Pax's face was tight. Most of the guys on the team, if not all, were easy to be around. We had a good sense of camaraderie and I worked hard to keep it up. But since Pax had joined us last season after Pittsburgh didn't renew his contract, he'd been a pain in our team's collective ass.

I had a feeling I knew why his last contract hadn't been renewed. It was because he was a divisive prick. He was a good player, though. Management wasn't done with him yet, so I just had to deal—we all did.

"I'm sure you can afford to retire, Your Highness," he said.

There was an undercurrent to his voice that I didn't like. "Watch it, dude."

He turned to look at me, his shirt still off and his chest puffed out. "I'm not your dude, *dude*."

I considered him. I was in a foul enough mood that punching him in the face seemed like a good idea right now. A *really* good idea.

"Woah," Reggie said to Pax. He stepped up beside me. "You need to watch your mouth. Chase's still got a good five inches on you. *Dude*."

Pax smiled at that. "I'm not afraid of His Highness." He bobbed his chin at Reggie. "You either, Old Man."

"Why's that? Because you only have half a damn brain?" Reggie smiled and cracked his knuckles. Reggie *was* old, but he was also crazy. If he did indeed have half a brain, Pax would shut his mouth quick.

"'Cause you two have lost your bite." Pax looked at us both in a challenge.

"Did you sprinkle your cereal with PCP this morning?" I asked. "'Cause I'm not really sure why you're starting this shit with your own teammates."

Reggie crossed his arms, his enormous biceps bulging, waiting to hear the cornerback's response.

"Are you gonna run off and tell Coach?" Pax asked,

mocking me. "Because *that* wouldn't surprise me one bit."

"What the fuck?" I asked him, my voice rising. "What's your *problem*?"

"You're my problem. *Dude.* Maybe not everybody's thrilled that this is the Chase Layne show twenty-four-seven."

"So go somewhere else—that is, if anybody'll take you," I said. I balled my hand into a fist, but a taunt was as far as I was willing to go. *He isn't worth it.*

A smug grin spread over Pax's face, making me feel sick to my stomach. What the fuck was up with this guy?

"Oh, I got somebody to take me all right." He motioned to his chest and down the rest of his body. "All of me."

Reggie turned to me. "Maybe it was LSD he sprinkled on his cereal. Dude's trippin'."

"Seriously. What the fuck are you talking about, Pax?" I asked.

"Jessica says 'hi'." He grinned at me again.

"Jessica? As in Jessica, my *wife*?" I looked at him, but all I could think about was my mother. *"Of course there's somebody else."*

No. No fucking way. Not my cornerback. She wouldn't.

Pax chuckled and beamed at me in triumph. "The very same."

That was the last thing I heard before I went after him and everything went black. And Reggie screaming for the other guys to come. Quick.

"YOU CAN'T SUSPEND me for two weeks, sir." I looked at Wes, my coach, desperately. "He's sleeping with my *wife*. He taunted me about it in the *locker room*. He's lucky he's not in the hospital." Pax had been treated and released by our team physician. He had a broken nose and some other nasty cuts and bruises.

Like I gave a fuck.

"No," Wes said. "*You're* lucky he's not in the hospital." He looked more tired than usual, as if the bags under his eyes had doubled in size.

I blew out a deep breath. "Jessica's leaving me for him." I called her after the fight with Pax and she'd admitted everything, not sounding sorry in the least. "He taunted me about it in public, in front of my *team-mate*, and I'm the one who's getting suspended? That's fucked up, Wes."

"Watch your mouth." Wes swore like a sailor, but he

didn't tolerate his players cursing. "You broke his nose, Chase. You have to be disciplined."

"What're we going to do about *him*? This is our last chance for a Super Bowl title. *My* last chance. And Pax is toxic. He wants to rip this team apart."

Wes looked at me calmly. "I can't suspend him for what he's done off the field. Adultery is not a criminal offense. What I *can* do is see if Tim will consider cutting him loose early. We can't have someone like him on the team—I agree with you about that—but it's not my decision."

Tim was the team owner. "Okay," I said. That was as much as I could ask for at this point.

"So…" Wes just sat there for a minute, gathering his thoughts. He didn't talk a lot, and he chose his words sparingly when he was forced to. "Jessica."

I nodded at him. "It's true."

"You two working it out?"

I laughed. "There's not a lot left to work out."

"Are you filing?"

I gritted my teeth. "She said she's going to do it this week."

Wes sat back and studied me. "You okay, son?"

"Yes." I sat there for a second. "No."

"You know the press is going to be all over this. Your

suspension, your divorce, and her, uh…new relationship."

"Yup." I looked at him grimly. The sports press in Boston was rabid. They would analyze it to death. "What're you going to say about Pax?"

"Nothing, if I can help it." Wes shrugged. "Just that he's on the injury list, you're suspended for violating team rules and that I have no further comment."

I grunted. "That's not gonna fly."

"It'll do for now—until I figure out what I *have* to tell them." He studied my face. "Is Jessica taking this public?"

"Probably." I felt numb inside.

"I'll talk to Tim, and I'll do the press conference after that. You take it easy. Take time to lie low. Work out at home. Maybe don't leave the house too much. Hopefully, we can keep the fact that Pax is involved private for now."

I nodded at Wes. "We'll see. Pax didn't seem like he was trying to keep it a secret."

My coach looked grim. "What did Jessica say about that?"

She was excited that Pax had started a fight with me.

She told me she was thrilled that she was finally with a real man.

"Nothing, sir. Thank you," I said and quickly took my leave.

"I TOLD you to have Jess sign a prenup," my attorney said. Sitting out back by my pool, Mickey looked out of place. He had on a pinstriped suit with a crisp lavender shirt. His neatly trimmed white hair stood unnaturally still, even in the breeze.

In contrast, I wore a ripped Warriors T-shirt and a pair of basketball shorts. I hadn't shaved in three days.

"She saw you coming, Chase. Jesus." My attorney smoothed his impeccable pants. "So…what's going on with her, exactly? She's found a new food source in the form of Pax Unger?"

I nodded. "Appears that way."

"Who'd she hire for the divorce?" He looked grim.

"I don't know yet," I said.

"What exactly happened with you two?"

I shrugged. "She wanted to do a bunch of stuff that I wasn't supporting. So I guess she found someone who would get with her program."

"What program's that?"

"She wanted to do a reality show—based on us," I sighed. "She'd gotten an agent to pitch it to the networks and everything."

"You mean—like a *Real Housewives* sort of thing?" he asked.

I grunted. "More like a *Kendra Loves Hank* kind of thing. You know the one with the ex-Playboy playmate, her ex-NFL husband, and their kids?"

Mickey scrubbed his hand across his face. "I must've missed that one."

"Jessica wanted cameras in the house twenty-four-seven. She wanted us filmed going to dinner, fighting, the whole deal."

"Management would never agree to that," he said.

"Well, I know that, and you know that, but that didn't stop Jess from being angry when I said it was never going to happen. She said I was ruining her career."

"*Her* career?" Mickey coughed. "Why didn't she just ask *WRX* for her old sports reporter job back? Sounds like she needed something to do."

I'd met Jess when she was a rising sports reporter for a local news station. She was smart. Focused. Tenacious. She was like a female version of me. I remember the first time I saw her—tall with long legs, dark hair cascading down her back. Incredible tits…that she'd subsequently defiled with too-large, fake-looking implants. "That's not what she wanted. That wasn't enough," I said. "She wanted a show about *her.* She kept talking about the Jessica Layne brand."

"Her *brand*?" He looked stymied. "I don't think she's exactly a good role model."

"She *did* go to Brown," I said, a little defensively.

"I didn't say she was dumb," Mickey said. "I just don't think she's a nice person. No offense, son."

I sighed. "None taken. You want a beer?"

Mickey nodded. "I could do a beer." He watched as I went to the outside refrigerator on my shaded patio. "All this wasn't enough for her?" he asked, gesturing around my setup—the enormous in-ground pool, the hot tub, the waterfall. "And why no kids?"

"She liked the money," I said. "But she wants to be famous in her own right. And she'd actually started bargaining with me about the kid thing. She never wanted to have one because she was worried about her figure. But if I'd have said yes to a series deal, she would've finally said yes to a kid." I took a large swig of beer. "So she could be filmed being mother of the year."

My attorney grimaced. "Real piece of work, Chase. A real piece of work. She's going to try to soak you. You know that, right?"

I shook my head. "Let her. I don't even care. And good riddance."

He was quiet for a minute, nursing his beer. "I'm surprised you punched the guy—Pax. Doesn't seem like you, going and doing something that would get you suspended."

It was out of character for me, and I didn't do "out of character".

"But I guess you had to," Mickey continued. "Somebody sleeps with your wife—even if you don't even like your wife—you have to punch him."

"That's sort of what I was thinking. If you could call it thinking."

Mickey patted my shoulder. "It's okay, son. We'll deal with Jessica. We'll make this whole thing go away."

I took another swallow of beer, wishing that was somehow true.

OF COURSE, Jessica would not go quietly. I hadn't spoken with her directly, per Mickey's orders, but he was dealing with the high-powered divorce lawyer she'd hired. Jessica had a long list of demands.

"She wants the *house*?" I screamed into my cell phone. "And *half* my money? We were only married for two years, for Christ's sake. We don't have any kids."

"She won't get it—not all of it," Mickey said, calmly, "but she's probably looking at alimony because she quit her job to support your career."

I snorted and gripped my phone, close to shattering it. "That's a joke and you know it. Everybody knows it.

All she's done is gone shopping, decorate, and get her face blown up with filler. Our marriage was a two-year, all-expenses-paid luxury *vacation* for her, goddamn it."

"Chase." Mickey's voice bordered on soothing, which was a red flag for me. "She's gonna get a large chunk of your money. You need to wrap your head around that. Now, you can pay me to fight her—we can do all sorts of things to drag this out—but then you're going to spend a fuck-ton of money on legal fees. Which is fine by me." He chortled. "But seriously, if you agree to at least some of what she's asking for, she'll probably settle. I think she wants to be done with this quick."

"Why do you think that?"

He was silent for a second. "Because her lawyer told me so."

"And why is that?"

Another pause. "Because she wants to get married again. As soon as possible."

I surprised myself by laughing. I just sat on the couch and laughed and laughed.

CHAPTER 4

CHASE

A few days later, my doorbell rang. I sat up. *Shit.* I'd been wearing the same pair of sweats, doing nothing but drinking beer and eating Chinese delivery and pizza. I was camped out in my living room, the NFL Network on constantly, not even bothering to go to my bedroom to sleep.

But it was only seven a.m. and I hadn't ordered any Chinese food yet.

The doorbell rang again. *Double shit.* It was probably my mother.

I checked the security camera.

Then I threw the door open. "Shut up."

"No—*you* shut up," Eric said, coming in and giving me a hug. My agent pulled back, his nose wrinkling below his black, stylish rectangular glasses. "You smell. Worse than usual."

He looked me up and down, taking in the rumpled sweats, which contrasted garishly with his Armani suit. Then he turned and inspected my messy house. "You bringing man-town to the main living room? I like it," he said, his face breaking into a grin. He pushed past me and surveyed the empty takeout cartons, the beer bottles, the blankets and remote controls scattered everywhere haphazardly…

"Jessica would *not* approve," he said, clapping me on the back, "so I do."

"What're you doing here?" I asked. Eric rarely came up to Boston. He preferred Los Angeles, where there was sun. And women wearing a lot less clothing than they usually wore up here in New England.

He grinned at me. "I talked to Martha. She said she was worried about you. So I thought I'd come up and stage a man-tervention." His eyes flicked to my sweat-pants again and then my hair, which was most likely really messed up. "I can see I made a wise choice."

He threw his bag down and stalked into the kitchen. I followed, shuffling behind.

"You want a beer?" I asked.

"It's seven in the morning—four a.m. my time." Eric raised his eyebrows. "We're having coffee."

"*I'm* having beer."

He took out two mugs, ignoring me, and turned my Nespresso machine on. He eyed the sink filled with dirty dishes, then opened the fridge to find it mostly empty. "Your housekeeper off this week?"

"I think Jessica fired her," I mumbled.

Eric laughed, shaking his head. "She's bitter to the end."

"You can say that again."

Eric was still chuckling. He hated Jessica and seemed positively giddy that she'd packed up and left. "It's gonna be okay, I promise. We'll get this all straightened out."

He handed me a coffee, and I hated to admit it, but it tasted great. Even better than beer.

Eric eyed me over his mug. "Why're you so upset? You haven't even *liked* her for the past year and a half."

I scrubbed my hands over my face. "I'm not upset about Jess."

"Then why're you such a wreck? What's with the sweatpants and the beer?"

"Football," I said and shuffled back out toward the couch. "I'm upset about football."

"Ah. Football. I should have known." Eric sat down next to me, moving some empty food cartons so he could put his feet up on the coffee table. "Wes handled the press conference well. He never gives anything away. Christ, those reporters must hate him."

I laughed. "They'd hate him if he wasn't so good at his job. He's going to try to keep the fight quiet for as long as possible. But Pax's coming back to practice soon. Someone's going to get a picture of his mangled face and put it all together. Unless Jessica lays it all out for them first." I was surprised she hadn't released a statement announcing our split and that I'd beaten up her new lover. That was exactly the sort of drama she loved.

"I talked to Mickey…" Eric's voice trailed off.

I winced. "Did he breach his attorney-client privilege again?"

My friend nodded.

"So you know that Jessica wants to get married to Pax? Soon?"

He nodded again. "You're not upset about that?"

"Nah." I was pretty sure those two deserved each other.

Eric watched my face. "But…you're upset about what it's going to do to the team?"

I could see the sympathy in Eric's eyes. He knew me too well. "Yes."

"Okay," Eric said. "You're suspended for another full week after this, right? And there's no word as to whether the Warriors are going to cut Pax loose?"

"Yes," I mumbled. "To both."

"You're going to have to deal with him sooner rather than later."

I groaned. "I thought you were here to cheer me up."

Eric sighed. "There's also a crap-ton of reporters outside your house, in case you didn't notice."

"That's what the pizza guy said." I curled up into a ball, wishing that my coffee would magically transform into a beer and that none of this had ever happened. To me.

Suspended. Humiliated in front of my teammates.

"What're you worried about, Chase?" Eric asked.

I squinted at him. "That might be the stupidest fucking question ever."

He crossed his legs, his elegant suit out of place amidst the man-squalor. "It's not a stupid question. I'm your agent, remember? Which means you pay me a lot of money to think of things you might not. To look out for you and your best interests. To consider every angle. Remember when I told you not to marry Jessica?"

"Yep. I remember. Everyone seems to be reminding me these days."

Eric sighed. "The point is you should have listened to me then. So please listen to me now. Let's go through the steps."

I sighed and shot him a menacing look. "Seriously?"

"I'm totally serious. We need to think this through. What are you *specifically* worried about?" Eric asked.

I knew Eric well enough to realize that he wasn't going to leave me alone until I played this silly game with him, so I answered. "I'm *specifically* worried that my team isn't going to respect me anymore. That I'm not going to be able to lead them because they've lost faith in me."

"And why are you worried that they've lost faith in you?" he asked.

"That's another stupid fucking question."

"Just answer it," he insisted.

"I'm worried that everybody's going to think that I have no dick because my wife left me for a teammate— the worst teammate I've got. And that Pax's going to try to rally them all against me, because that's the kind of shit-starter he is."

Eric's brow furrowed. "He doesn't care about the team?"

"He's fucking the quarterback's wife. What do *you* think?"

"Tim'll cut him," he said confidently.

"Pax is an asshole, but he's a strong defensive player," I countered. "We need him more than he needs us right now."

Eric shrugged. "He needs a paycheck, Chase. Just like the rest of us."

"He seems to think he can do whatever—or whoever —he wants."

"We'll deal with Pax. Let's see what management does first." Eric seemed to concentrate on his coffee. "Either way, we have to face the whole thing head on. So let's break it down. Even though you're glad Jessica's gone, you're worried about what your team's going to think of you because you're a cuckold."

I looked at him grimly. "What the fuck does that mean?"

"It's a Shakespearean term, buddy. It means you were cheated on. Duped. Humiliated. And everybody knows it."

I grimaced. "Is that supposed to make me feel better?"

"No," Eric said carefully, "it's supposed to help us identify the real problem so we can come up with a solution."

"I don't think there's a solution to having your wife sleep with your teammate and then leave you for him. In the public eye. With a very large chunk of your money."

"You're right," Eric conceded. "But there *are* ways to make you feel like you're back on top. To maintain your team's respect—but if I'm being honest with you, I know those guys. Your teammates worship you. They'd do anything for you. I don't think that's going to change just because of what Jessica did."

I shook my head. "I don't know...they won't see me the same way." Thick misery descended on me again. I could deal with everything that had happened, but I didn't want to lose the trust and camaraderie I'd worked so hard to build with my teammates. I didn't want them to doubt me, doubt my judgment.

Doubt my *balls*.

They were counting on me, just like I counted on them. This was supposed to be our year, and now everything was on the precipice of going to hell.

"You just need to seem like you're still on top. That's all," Eric said. He never failed in his supreme confidence in me. "You guys are in good shape to make the playoffs. You'll be the NFL Player of the Year. I know it. You've been working hard for this your whole life. Don't let Jessica fuck it up for you."

He stood up and started pacing. "You show your team you haven't faltered, their belief in your leadership won't falter, either."

I ran my hand over my head; I could already feel my crew cut growing out. "How do you propose I do that? Am I supposed to go back to practice next week with a big grin on my face? Fake it until I make it or something? That's fucking stupid."

"Jessica wants the house, right?"

I nodded.

"So let her have it," he continued. "Let's go find a sweet condo in downtown Boston. The press is going to be following you. Let the public see you out and about, looking fine, moving on. That sends a message. And I'm going to get you a smoldering hot girlfriend. *Blistering* hot." Eric had a manic gleam in his eye. "We'll stick *that* in Jessica's pipe and let her smoke it."

"Um…Eric? I hate to break it to you, but you can't stick my non-existent girlfriend into Jess's non-existent pipe," I said. I didn't know what the hell he was talking about. "I don't have a girlfriend. I don't *want* a girlfriend. I just barely got rid of my wife, who was a Grade A pain in my ass. I'm not ready for anything else. Not even close."

He smiled at me. "You don't have to be ready. You just have to look like you are."

"I don't understand." Maybe Eric was finally losing his touch.

"I'm going to *hire* a girlfriend for you. For show." He'd pulled out his phone and his fingers were already flying over it, tapping away.

"I think you've officially lost it, buddy. I thought it was just me, but now I'm pretty sure it's you, too." I looked at him as if he had three heads, but he was ignoring me.

Eric feverishly scrolled through his phone. "Do you remember Cole Bryson?"

I stared at him. "What the *fuck* are you talking about now?"

"Cole Bryson—that dude who owns the Thunder?"

Cole Bryson was a billionaire investment guy I knew from Boston. He also owned a Bruins farm team, the Rhode Island Thunder. I liked Cole, but I hadn't talked to him in ages. "Yeah, I know Bryson. What the hell does he have to do with anything?"

Eric looked up from his phone and smiled. "A buddy of mine just went to Cole's wedding. He married an *escort*. He hired her and then they fell in love. No shit. My friend said the bride and all of her escort friends were smoking hot. So I'm getting one for you. A cute one."

My headache was back in full force. "Eric...shut the fuck up." The last thing I needed in my life right now was a hooker.

He ignored me, his fingers flying back over the phone. "No way. I'm going to get the number for the agency. I'm hiring the hottest woman on the planet to be your girlfriend. She's going to have an airtight confidentiality agreement, Chase. And a rocking bod—with *real* boobs. I'll ask specifically for that. Jess'll hate it."

I opened my mouth to object, but he cackled, cutting me off. "I can't wait to see the look on Jessica's face," he said gleefully.

And with that, he started talking on the phone before I could stop him. Before I could ask him if he'd actually gone completely, utterly nuts.

CHAPTER 5

AVERY

"It's a high-profile assignment," Elena was saying, but it was as if I couldn't hear her.

Fifty thousand dollars. That'd been the first thing out of her mouth. After that, my knees had buckled and I had to sit down. Everything else she'd said was fuzzy.

"Avery." She cleared her throat. "Look at me, honey."

I looked at the madam, finding her spiky, frosted hair and maroon lipstick strangely comforting. I'd never figured out how Elena had gotten into the business when she looked like a soccer mom from Wellesley. Then some of the other girls had told me that she actually *was* a soccer mom from Wellesley…who just happened to run an escort service.

"Are you okay?" Elena asked, breaking my reverie.

I swallowed hard over the newly formed lump in my throat. "That's a lot of money."

She nodded. "I know. I want this client. He could be a *huge* source of confidential, big-money referrals for me. And I know that kind of money would be life-changing for you."

I couldn't even wrap my brain around it. With fifty thousand dollars in my pocket, we wouldn't get evicted. Ever. I could afford to send Lila to rehab. I could stop hooking. I could take classes and get a different job—one that didn't involve a stranger's hands all over me.

I shivered.

"Are you up for this?" the madam asked.

"Of course," I said immediately. "But why me? Why not one of the regular girls?"

Elena smiled. "The client wants the cleanest and the hottest girl I have. That's you, all day long. You'll have to have your drug and STD testing updated, of course," she said. "Are either one of those going to be a problem?"

"No," I said, my voice hoarse.

"Have you been taking your pills every day?"

I nodded. One of the contract requirements was that we took birth control. The agency provided it.

The madam crossed her elegant legs and folded her hands together. "The escort business isn't for everyone,

Avery. You have to look at it analytically and weigh your needs against your limits."

I looked at her. "I *need* this job."

"Well then—it's yours." She smiled. "This is sort of a... different situation. It isn't a straight-up call."

I nodded at her, pretending I understood, even though I didn't.

"The client is Chase Layne. The Warriors quarterback."

My jaw dropped.

"Are you familiar with him?"

"Of course," I said breathlessly. Chase Layne was famous—he was the best quarterback in the NFL. He was also a celebrity. Drop-dead gorgeous, six-foot-five with coppery skin and big, gorgeous blue eyes, he was the face of more advertising campaigns than I could keep track of. When I'd seen him on the cover of gossip magazines, he'd always seemed untouchable, perfect. "But I thought he was married!"

"You're not up on the news, huh?" Elena asked.

As I currently had no phone, no computer, no television, and couldn't afford to buy magazines, the answer to that was a solid *no*. "I don't have time," I mumbled.

A flash of knowing sympathy crossed Elena's face. All of the girls who worked for her needed the money, and she knew it. "The story just broke, but only some of it's in the news. His wife left him recently. And Chase has been suspended from the Warriors for two weeks."

"Why?" I asked.

"*This* part's confidential—Chase's agent just told me," she said conspiratorially. "Jessica Layne's been having an affair with one of the teammates, Pax Unger. Chase found out and went after him. He broke Pax's nose. The team hasn't made that part public."

"Yikes," I said.

"'Yikes' is right. Chase is going back to practice in another week. The press has been hounding him. His agent has decided that, because his public image is going to take a beating, he needs to launch a preemptive counterattack. New house, new girlfriend, same great attitude. Obviously, he doesn't have time to meet someone new and fall in love—so that's where we come in."

Elena got up and grabbed a garment bag, hustling into the endless racks of clothes she kept in the office for our assignments. "His attorney has prepared a lengthy confidentiality agreement. You have to sign it and understand that these people mean business. You are going to act like his girlfriend, attend public events with him, and live in his home. The payment we've received is for one month. There's a renewal option if he wants to continue the arrangement. Are you okay with this so far?"

I nodded and watched, fascinated, as she assembled several gorgeous outfits for me. *The assignment could last longer than a month.* That meant more money. Lots more money and some actual, tangible room between me and the street.

Holy smokes. This is the opportunity of a lifetime.

"You can't ever reveal—not to anyone, not *ever*—that you were hired to do this. You can't tell your sister. You can't tell your best friend. You can't write a book about it or try to sell the story to *XYZ* or one of those other tabloids. If you ever do that, the contract is broken and they will come after you for every cent you earn, as well as damages. Understood?"

I nodded at her mutely. "I would never do that, Elena."

"I know. You're a good girl—probably too good to be working here, but everybody's got their reasons. And trust me, they're all good ones."

I bit my lip. I wanted this so badly, but my thoughts were going into overdrive. "Aren't you worried that the press is going to find out about me? A girlfriend from out of nowhere is going to make a lot of people curious —especially when it comes to Chase Layne."

Elena smiled at me. "I've got you covered. I had a high-profile client out in California recently. It taught me a thing or two about protecting my employee's identities. We'll have false identification prepared for you once you sign the contract. A new name with a new driver's license, birth certificate, etcetera. I'll have it ready for you later today."

She packed a conservative grey dress and some silky tank tops. "Another thing... When I spoke with Chase's agent, Eric, he was very clear about the image he wants you to project. Chase's ex was a television journalist—very flashy, with fancy nails, fake boobs and designer clothes. They want the opposite of that. No body-conscious clothes, not a lot of makeup... They just want you to look pretty. Innocent." She gave me a wry smile.

"Works for me."

Elena continued bustling about. "Your backstory is your parents are dead and you're an only child. From New Hampshire. You have family money. You've been looking for a job around Boston but haven't found anything promising yet. You met Chase at the Barnes and Noble in Harvard Square. There was an instant spark. He knew right away that you were a nice girl, unlike that cheater who just left him."

She put a sophisticated, expensive-looking black dress into the garment bag. "Your new name is Avery Brighton. And you have your whole, beautiful, sparkling life in front of you—with Chase Layne."

WITH THE SIGNING money Elena had given me, I paid my landlord for the next three months' rent as soon as I got home. It was a huge relief. Lila was nowhere to be found in the apartment, which was both a blessing and a curse. A blessing because I wouldn't have to lie to her face, which I genuinely sucked at. A curse because whatever she was out doing was probably something that she shouldn't.

I packed up the toiletries and personal items I needed and wrote her a note. *Dear Lila, I'm heading out of town for a while. Rent's taken care of. You can reach me at this number—for emergencies only!* I jotted down the number for the loaner phone Elena had given me, the one I wasn't supposed to make personal calls from. But I felt better leaving my sister with a way to contact me.

I wanted to remind Lila that she still needed to get a job, and beg her to keep the apartment tidy while I was gone, but I knew she'd just roll her eyes at that.

I swallowed back the bitter taste in my mouth as I folded the note. Because we had no television and no Internet connection, I hoped that Lila wasn't going to see pictures of me with Chase Layne anytime soon. I was walking a fine line between taking care of her and being taken advantage of by her.

I loved my sister, but I didn't trust her—I couldn't. Lila would go nuts if she heard how much money I was making. And then she would find a way to spend it—*all* of it—and then I'd be back to square one. Again.

Not this time.

I locked up the apartment and headed downstairs. There was a hired Town Car waiting for me. I slid into the backseat and relaxed against the clean interior. As the driver nodded at me politely and pulled down the street, I looked up at my apartment building. I was thrilled to be leaving it behind. I was also thrilled I was going to pretend to be someone else. I'd never taken a vacation, but aside from the fact that this was an escort assignment, it sounded like the ultimate escape.

Avery Banks has left the building, I thought, a little wildly.

Hello, Avery Brighton. I liked my new name. It was new and shiny, full of promise.

Everything that I wasn't.

CHAPTER 6

CHASE

"I can't believe you hired a hooker for me," I said, pacing around my kitchen. "This is a bad idea. Fucked up. I'm not one of those ballplayers. I don't want my reputation getting completely ruined."

"Will you relax? No one's going to know she's a hooker!" Eric was looking through my refrigerator, which had recently been stocked by the maid service he'd hired. "And for the record, she's an escort, not a hooker. This is going to work. Trust me. This will give you the confidence you need, and you'll go down in history as one of the best quarterbacks that ever played. Just like you've always wanted."

I snorted and continued to pace. The house was immaculate again and was about to be listed by a real estate agent. Jessica had decided that she didn't want it, after all. She just wanted the proceeds of the sale. I had a few choice words for her about that, but I was keeping them to myself...for now. I didn't want to start a pissing contest with her.

"I don't want a prostitute—or an escort, or whatever —living with me," I said. The idea made me want to throw up.

"Relax. She's a nice girl, Chase."

I stopped pacing and threw up my arms. "How do you know?"

"Because I saw her picture. She looks very, *very* nice." Eric grinned at me. "I think you'll like her."

I cracked my knuckles, wishing that I was cracking Eric's face. I had no idea what this girl was going to be like. I was worried she was going to be user, or a smoker, or just a mess in general. "This better not turn into a disaster. I'm in enough trouble as it is. You need to keep her in line."

The grin slid off Eric's face. "You have to at least give her a chance," he said. "This isn't going to work if you keep acting like you have your period."

The doorbell rang and my stomach lurched. I sat down and buried my face in my hands. "I can't believe we're doing this. I seriously feel sick."

"For a big, tough quarterback, you're really being a pussy," Eric said, striding out to get the door.

I held my breath as I heard him exchange pleasantries with someone.

If she's a smoker, she's fired, was all I could think as I went out to meet her.

I rounded the corner and stopped dead in my tracks.

The escort—if this was, indeed, the escort—looked like she was in her early twenties. She had long, blond, wavy hair and a fresh face devoid of makeup. She was wearing a Dartmouth T-shirt and leggings. I could tell she had real boobs, just like Eric promised, and they were fantastic. She smiled at me nervously.

She was stunning, just in the T-shirt. She seemed innocent enough. Nice, even.

"I'm Avery," she said, that same nervous smile plastered to her face. Her voice was sweet with an undercurrent of anxiety, like she was trying to be pleasing.

I'm fucked. She was absolutely gorgeous. My cock, long dormant, actually twitched.

So. Fucking. Inconvenient.

I nodded at her. "Chase Layne."

And then I promptly left the room.

"GET OUT THERE and talk to her," Eric ordered.

I sat on my bed, playing *Madden*. "I'm busy."

"You're really being a dick," Eric said. "She's a nice girl. I have her all moved into the guest suite and unpacked. She's probably wondering what the fuck your problem is."

"Tell her she's my problem. And you, too," I snapped, trying to watch the screen.

Eric sighed. "The press already got pictures of her coming in and the driver carrying her suitcases. Look—" he shoved his phone in front of my face. "It's already online."

Mystery Woman Moves into Layne's Wellesley Home, the headline read on the *Gazette's* website.

"Don't they have some real news to report?" I snapped.

"Apparently not. They know about her. So that means she's in." Eric shoved my Xbox controller down and watched my face. "Which means it's game time. Get up."

I glared at my friend. "I don't have the energy for this. It was a mistake." All I wanted to do was get back to my couch, eat Chinese, and count the days until I could go back to practice. I wanted to sit around in a rage and lick my wounds. Alone. In my sweatpants.

"I don't want to babysit a hooker. I'm out."

"You can't be out," Eric said, exasperated. "Get *up*. As long as I'm your agent, and I'm involved in your career, I expect you to be successful. You want that, right? That's what all this boo-hooing's about, isn't it?"

I kept glaring at him.

"If you want to get back on top, you have to take that first step. You can't climb sitting down. So stick to the plan. And go take a shower, for Christ's sake."

After he left, my phone buzzed.

Jessica: who the f was that

Chase: I can't understand you when you don't speak English.

Jessica: the mystery woman at your house

I swallowed hard, picturing Jess and Pax tripping over themselves to get to the computer every time a Google Alert went off for my name.

Chase: My new girlfriend. She's pretty, huh?

Jessica: she looks boring but that's perf for you haha

Chase: And Pax is a douchebag so he's 'perf' for you HA HA HA!

Jessica: soooo glad i'm not near you right now

Chase: That makes two of us.

I sent her a smiling emoji and she didn't respond. Thank God.

Ten minutes later, I came out, showered and dressed in cargo shorts and a Warriors T-shirt. Avery was sitting on the couch next to Eric, watching what appeared to be one of my highlight reels, and listening carefully as my agent explained the different plays.

I stood in the doorway and watched them for a minute. She looked lovely and unassuming, not dull at all.

"What're you two doing?" I asked. It came out sharper than I'd intended. Hearing from Jessica had left me feeling pissed at the world.

Avery jumped and Eric winced. "We're reviewing plays, Chase. I thought it would be beneficial for Avery to get more familiar with your work."

"Turn it off," I snapped. "You don't need to do that."

Eric sighed. "I think it would be nice if she knew more about your record. That's all."

"You don't need to bore her to death." This girl was in my house because we'd asked her to come, but I didn't want her here. I didn't want to have to pretend, and I didn't want to deal with everyone asking me about her. I *also* didn't want to look at her eager, pretty face, and have to deal with whatever emotional baggage she was carrying. She was an escort. There *had* to be baggage.

"I'm a big fan of yours," Avery offered, her voice wobbly. She was blushing. "Eric was just explaining your record to me. I'd like to know more."

I stared at her reddening face, unable to respond.

"D-do you want to watch it with us?" she asked. I'd never seen such a pretty girl stammer before. She was the polar opposite of Jessica. If a guy wasn't eating out of Jess's hands within two minutes, she'd promptly drive a spiked high heel into his back.

"I've seen it," I said, backing out of the room.

Eric followed me to the kitchen. "Cut. The. Shit," he said, keeping his voice down, the look on his face incredulous. "Why're you being so *mean*? This girl didn't just show up here to be your groupie—we *hired* her. She's here on assignment. And unlike you, she's trying to be professional."

"*You* hired her, Eric. Not me."

He raked his hands through his hair, obviously frustrated. "If you want to fire her now and ask her to leave, go ahead. But that's on you."

I sighed and gripped the edge of my island as if I was holding on for dear life.

"Do you really think this is going to work?" I asked him. "Jess already texted me. She's reacting. I don't know if this is going to be worth dealing with her shit, too."

"If Jess is off balance, that means this was the right move," Eric said. "You're the bigger story. They'll lose the advantage. And then all you have to do is play ball and lead your team."

"That's all I want," I said.

"Then get out of your own way." Eric jerked his thumb toward the living room. "She's waiting for you. I'll be in here."

I looked toward the living room. "But what do I *say?*" I asked.

Eric groaned. "Dude, you're hopeless. That's it. We're going out. We need help. *You* need help." Shaking his head, he headed back toward the living room.

"What're you doing?" I asked.

He didn't even bother to turn around. "Taking care of business, Chase. Shots. Shots make everything better. Now go put on some goddamned jeans. You look like a frat boy in those cargo shorts."

AVERY

I heard Eric and Chase arguing in the kitchen. I wanted to hide. Actually, I wanted to run away and never look back.

This was a disaster. Chase Layne *hated* me.

The quarterback was a tall, gorgeous, hulking wall of muscle, and he *hated* me.

It was clear he was out of my league, but he didn't have to be so mean about it. I sat there, picking at invisible lint on my shirt and feeling miserable, until Eric came back in.

"Hey," Eric said. He smiled at me apologetically. "Sorry. Chase is, er…acting up. He's been through a lot lately."

"S'okay." I nodded at him. The truth was, Chase had rebuffed me so hard I practically had bruises. "I'm not what he was…expecting?" I felt my face start to flush. The star quarterback probably had a type. Clearly, I was not it.

Eric let out a bark of laughter. "I'm pretty sure you're every breathing man's type. That's not the problem." He smiled at me kindly. "The *problem* is that this scenario was my idea. I hired you because I believe that you'll help strengthen Chase's image. But he's not thrilled about it. It's not personal, so please don't take it that way."

"Would you like to me to leave for a little while so you two can figure it out, or he has more time to adjust to the idea?"

Quite frankly, being as far away from Chase Layne as I could sounded like a great idea. I was pretty sure that I disgusted him. Maybe he could set his agent straight, and I could get out of here with at least some shred of dignity left.

I was quickly losing hope about the money. I tried not to think about it.

The agent shook his head. "No way. We've cleared you, we've signed the contract, and the press is already posting pictures of you. You're in. So go get changed—we're going to have drinks and then we're going to dinner. The three of us."

"Chase is onboard for this?" I asked.

"Absolutely."

I must have looked worried, because Eric reached out and patted my arm. "We'll have fun. I *promise*."

I went and changed into a simple black dress and sandals. All of the clothes that Elena had packed for me were expensive and well made. This dress probably cost more than I made in a month waitressing at the *Sizzling Ranch*. I looked at myself in the mirror, smoothing the fabric. The dress looked good. It hugged my curves and showed off my legs without being too sexy. I wondered what it would feel like to own a dress like this, to have it in my closet. *To have paid for it with my own money.*

Just wearing it gave me some much needed confidence. I put on a little mascara and some lip gloss. I pushed my boobs up and fluffed my hair. Chase Layne might hate me, but I wasn't going to give up this assignment without a fight.

Now if I could just get him to talk to me.

I found Chase and Eric in the kitchen. Eric was lining up exotic-looking shots on the island and he'd put out a bowl of freshly cut limes. The agent grinned at me when I came through, his eyes drifting down my body. "You look lovely, Avery."

Chase turned to me. His eyes stayed firmly on my face. "Hey."

I smiled at him tentatively. "Hey." I turned back to Eric. "Shots?"

Eric's eyes sparkled mischievously. "That's right. They're called A Kick in the Crotch. Vodka, blue curacao and cranberry juice."

"They're purple," I said, wrinkling my nose.

"*A Kick in the Crotch?*" Chase looked menacingly at his friend.

Eric shrugged. "Sometimes you need one."

"You're seriously an asshole. You know that, right?" Chase asked him, grabbing a drink.

"I know that. Right." Eric grinned at him. "And for the lady." He handed me a shot, which I held carefully.

"It's not going to bite you," Chase said. There was a note of sympathy in his voice.

I felt my shoulders relax a little. "I'm not a big drinker."

Chase actually smiled at me. "I'm not usually, either. At least, not during training. So we can be partners in relative sobriety. We'll leave the puking up to Eric." He looked as if he'd relaxed a bit since our last encounter, and I felt the nervous ache in my stomach subside slightly.

Eric knocked back his shot and shoved a lime into his mouth. "We have a driver," he said, through the lime. "It might very well be a boot-and-rally sort of night."

Chase tipped his glass toward mine. "Cheers. To Eric puking."

I laughed and, knowing full well that I had no idea what I was getting into, drank my first A Kick in the Crotch shot ever.

CHAPTER 7

AVERY

Someone must have stuffed sand in my mouth.

At least, that's what it felt like. I opened my eyes slowly, aware only of my dry mouth and the pounding in my head. *Welcome to being kicked in the crotch.* I gripped the bed, which was threatening to tilt.

I scrunched one eye open, trying to figure out where I was.

All I saw was the enormous, hulking form of a shirtless Chase Layne snoring next to me, his bronze skin glinting in the early morning sun.

I shut my eyes tightly again, which only made my head hurt worse. *Fuck.* I moved a little and felt how sore my whole body was.

Fuck was right.

The last thing I remembered lucidly was drinking margaritas at a Mexican restaurant in Harvard Square. Everything was hazy after that. I only could recall snippets.

Chase and I dancing on a table in a club.

A *club*? When the hell did we go to a club? Since when did I *dance*? How the hell did Chase dance on a table without crushing it? And when had he actually started tolerating my presence?

Chase taking a body shot from between my boobs.

Chase with his hands on my ass, grinding his thick erection against me on the dance floor.

I felt my face flush. I gathered the sheet tightly around me.

Chase naked underneath me, a look of shocked pleasure on his face, his eyes burning into mine.

Holy mother of God. There was more news than Chase's toleration of my presence.

We'd had sex.

More was coming back to me now. I cringed underneath the blankets. An image of myself riding him, my back arched, my boobs bouncing in his face, suddenly appeared in my brain, and I winced. I'd been, er...largely uninhibited once I'd drank God only knew what and we'd taken our clothes off. I remembered that much.

I screamed his name when I came. Hollered it.

He was just so *big*. I certainly remembered *that*.

"Holy fuck, Chase. YES! Fuck me just like that, baby! Right there!"

I couldn't believe I'd said—screamed—that. What the actual *fuck*?

We'd had sex, and I'd liked it. A lot. I'd orgasmed with him more than once. That might be the most shocking discovery of all.

Another image came back to me in a heated flash—the way he'd gripped my hips and his big blue eyes had locked with mine. He'd emptied himself into me and I'd shattered around him, my pussy sucking him dry in pure female triumph.

I thought he hated me. Was it a hate fuck?

If it was, I might have to try it again. It seriously worked for me.

My face flamed, and I pulled the sheet up over my head. I was so fucking mortified. Yes, I was an escort. *His* escort. No, I was neither a virgin nor a prude—I didn't think. But grinding my clit against a guy's shaft and screaming my head off when he made me come so hard I couldn't see straight? A guy I barely knew?

These things were not exactly my style.

Neither was letting someone take a body shot from between my boobs, but apparently, all bets had been off last night.

I'd been hired by Chase Layne for a job, and Elena had made it clear: I was here for the sex as much as anything else. *If Chase wanted.* But I'd just met the star quarterback yesterday, and he hadn't even seemed to *like* me. And I was pretty sure that I didn't like him—or it was at least clear to me that I shouldn't. I couldn't. He was so far out of my league, I couldn't even see his stadium from my seat.

But all of that had clearly changed—or just been drunkenly ignored—after multiple purple shots, margaritas, a body shot, and God knew what else. Maybe if Eric kept Chase and me drunk the entire time I was here, we'd get along just fine.

But I hadn't slept with him last night because I felt like I had to. It wasn't awkward like my other assignments, where I'd waited, dreading the John's first touch.

I'd had *fun* last night. I was drunk and when Chase had pressed all those big muscles against me, it'd made me horny as all hell. I remembered pulling him into my room and ripping his shirt off, gleefully running my hands down his enormous chest, feeling like I'd just opened the best Christmas present *ever*.

He rolled his massive body over and threw his arm across my chest. I held my breath, not daring to move. Part of me considered getting up and running. Maybe he wouldn't remember everything that happened.

Another part of me contemplated staying and playing with his enormous erection, which jutted against my thigh. If I was being honest with myself—which I genuinely tried *not* to be while on assignment—I really wanted to take another ride on Chase Layne's massive manhood. Just to see if it was as awesome as I remembered. I'd never screamed like that before. The pleasure I'd felt was utterly new to me. My thighs shuddered just thinking about it, which somehow made my head hurt worse.

Had I retained my sense of humor this morning, I would've laughed. Instead, I pulled the sheet off my face so I could breathe.

Chase opened one eye and looked at me. "Hey." He sounded vaguely surprised.

"Morning." I forced myself to smile at him, even though it killed my head.

He opened his other eye and looked as though he were trying to clear the fog from his brain. "Well...I guess we broke the ice last night."

I wanted to dive back under the covers. "Um, yep. We sure did."

He took his arm off me and quickly took his erection back to his side of the bed. He gave me an embarrassed smile. "Sorry about that."

I felt cold without his body touching mine. "It's okay.

You were asleep." *It's okay. We fucked each other's brains out last night, remember? Don't worry about a little morning pokey-pokey!*

Again, if I'd been capable, I would've giggled. Instead, I said nothing, and things instantly went back to awkward and miserable between myself and Chase Layne.

He sat up and gave me a wooden smile. "Well…gotta go hit the gym." He grabbed his underwear from somewhere under the sheets and pulled a T-shirt over his head.

And then he practically ran out of the room.

I might be the worst escort *ever.*

CHAPTER 8

CHASE

I can't believe I fucked her. *I just had to go and fuck her.* That had never been the plan. She was for show, not to shove my dick into.

Of course, my traitorous dick twitched at the thought. *It* wanted to go shove itself all sorts of places after last night. *Avery's pussy, Avery's mouth, between Avery gorgeous, round tits...*

I grabbed some heavier weights to punish myself and tried to stop obsessing about her. Hot images from last night kept flashing in my mind, but I didn't feel right about what we'd done. Last night I'd felt very, *very* right —but in the light of day, I was nothing but ashamed.

I'd taken advantage of this girl. Avery was here because she was on a job. I didn't believe for a second that she was an escort because she enjoyed it. She was too young, too pretty, too *innocent*. She must really need the money. *She was as vulnerable as she could have been, and I'd preyed on her.* My gut twisted at the thought.

But last night, once I stopped being a dick, she'd seemed like she was having fun. And even as shy as Avery had been when she'd first shown up, she'd lost all inhibition once we'd gotten back to her room. She'd ridden my cock and bossed me around like a pro, and I'd loved every second of it.

That's because she is *a pro.* My gut twisted again. *I fucked a prostitute.*

I couldn't believe it.

I felt sick—not because I thought bad things about Avery and what she did for work—not at all. It was because I felt like I'd exploited her. I was not one of those pro athletes who thought I could take what I wanted, when I wanted. That wasn't how I operated. I thought prostitution was dangerous, ugly, and degrading to women.

Says the guy who just hired a hooker.

I added more weights, grunting as I did another chest press. Never in my wildest dreams had I thought I'd end up sleeping with her. I thought I was above taking advantage of people. But I'd fucked her brains out last night, and I'd enjoyed every abandoned, debaucherous second.

Worse than that? I'd enjoyed running my hands through her long blond hair. The power I'd felt when she came so hard she screamed my name. Waking up next to her warm body—before I realized how badly I'd messed up.

I fucking hated myself this morning.

But before I could do more punishing presses, my phone started to blow up.

First was a text from Reggie. *That is a seriously hot girl,* he wrote. *You're the man.*

It buzzed again—a text from Trevor, one of my defenseman. *Who's the blonde?* he wrote with a winking emoji. *She have a sister?*

I grunted as my phone continued to vibrate.

Be prepared for Jessica to lash out, Mickey wrote. *But who cares? That girl's gorgeous.* Even Mickey included a winking emoji. Christ.

So much for laying low, wrote my coach, Wes. *Nice to see you looking relaxed, though. But maybe lay off the binge-drinking in public when the season's about to start.* There was no winking emoji.

I expect to meet this young lady sooner rather than later, Martha wrote. *Your mother's always the last to know, I guess.* No winking emoji.

I grimaced and did a quick Internet search of my name. Sure enough, there was picture after picture from last night posted to Instagram and Twitter. Images of me with different fans, grinning and holding various alcoholic beverages. I barely remembered any of it.

What was consistent in each picture was my smile and my grip around Avery. My arm was locked securely around her waist in each shot. She smiled next to me for an endless stream of photos, looking genuinely happy. I remembered the feel of my palm against her hip, pulling her to me. I loved the way holding her felt.

I scrolled through more pictures.

We were just pretending. Why does it look so real?

"You're really nice to your fans," she'd said after we'd posed for yet another shot. "I think it's sweet."

Jessica had grown to hate the fans. After a while, she'd thought she was above them. She just didn't get it.

"The fans are the best part," I'd said. "Without them, it doesn't mean a whole lot."

Avery smiled at me then, and I felt as if I was seeing her real smile. Part of me had softened toward her in spite of my better judgment.

And then I'd had another drink. And another.

After we finished at the restaurant, Eric had insisted that we go to a hot new club in the Theater District. That's when all the trouble had started. He'd called ahead, and we'd been let in immediately, cutting the long line that snaked down Tremont Street. A starstruck hostess had ushered us up a winding staircase to a VIP booth. Avery's eyes were wide as she'd taken in the mass of writhing bodies on the dance floor, the multi-colored lights bouncing off the chandeliers.

I leaned over to her. "Do you like clubs?" I'd asked, genuinely curious. I personally hated them. I danced like Frankenstein—or so Jess had told me.

"I've never been anywhere like this," she'd said, gesturing around and laughing self-consciously. "But I'm pretty sure it's not my scene."

I wanted to pull her against me to protect her—*from the dancers below? From the swirling lights?*—but I didn't feel like I had the right. "We don't have to stay long." The waitress brought over a bottle of vodka, different juices, and limes. I took another look at Avery, the way her hair tumbled past her shoulders as she laughed at something Eric shouted over the music. I grunted to myself, feeling the low pull of desire in my belly. She was undeniably gorgeous, and even better than that, she wasn't annoying...she was nice. Sweet. And now that we'd both relaxed a little, she was easy to be around.

I didn't make a conscious decision about it then. About her. I made a conscious decision to drink enough to *not* make a conscious decision—which, in dude logic, is essentially the same thing.

We all did another shot, and then things started to get blurry.

Avery excused herself to go to the ladies' room, and I watched her. Her hair swung as she timidly made her way through the crowd. Every guy she walked by checked her out, looking at her as though she were a cupcake they wanted to devour. I clenched my hands into fists. *I should've gone with her...* If one of these drunk fucks touched her, they were going to get pummeled, courtesy of Chase Layne.

The booze was making me more aggressive than usual, which was saying something. I stood up, getting ready to follow her.

"Chase," Eric interrupted me, "you're doing better, but you need to touch her more. People are seeing you together for the first time. This needs to seem real."

"I'm getting along with her," I said, defensively, trying to see her through the crowd. "I'm making an effort."

Eric snorted. "You make it sound like such a chore. She's *gorgeous*, dude. And sweet. If she wasn't an escort, you'd totally be into this girl."

"She's cute," I admitted warily.

He shook his head. "Maybe you've had so much

pussy thrown at you over the years that you're immune to her."

"I don't go after pussy that's thrown at me. That's desperate, and I don't do desperate."

Eric held up his hands to stop me. "Just dance with her. Act like she's your girlfriend, dammit."

"*Okay*, dammit."

Eric motioned to the server and had her pour us two more shots. I knocked mine back and went to find Avery.

"Where're you going?" Eric yelled after me, over the music.

"To find my girlfriend." I jerked my thumb toward the throng of dudes in skinny pants and too much hair gel. "Gotta protect her from the natives."

I *did* want to find her. I'd brought her here; she was my responsibility. I didn't want to tell Eric that I was starting to like her; it was a) none of his damned business, and b) I didn't want to hear him praise himself and say "I told you so" again so soon. I pushed my way through the crowd, smiling and nodding when I was recognized. I didn't stop until I was parked outside the ladies' room.

A frizzy, strawberry blonde stumbled out, wearing a sequined tank top and too much lipstick. She almost fell over when she spotted me. "Chase *Layne*?" she yelped. "Shut the fuck up!"

I grinned at her. "Can you do me a favor?"

The girl started twisting her coarse hair, her eyes glittering. I'd seen that look before—often from a defensive end who was about to tackle me.

She grinned back at me. "Oh *yeah*, I can. You betcha."

I jerked my thumb toward the ladies' room. "Can you go ask my girlfriend if she's okay? She's blond. Black dress. On the taller side."

The girl looked crestfallen for a second, but then she obediently ducked back into the bathroom. Women had been throwing themselves at me my whole life. I never once took one up on it. I was a big, star quarterback, but I was *not* a hookup kind of dude. What I'd said to Eric was the truth. I didn't do desperate. Not only because I didn't have to, but because to me, desperate was the opposite of sexy.

"Found her," the strawberry blonde said, her bottom lip jutting out. She had Avery in tow. My escort tentatively smiled at me when she found me guarding the door to the ladies' room.

"Hey," she said.

"Hey yourself." I grinned at her and then turned to the other girl. "Thank you. That was really nice."

She perked up a little and shrugged. "No problem. Can we take a picture?"

"Sure. D'ya mind if my girlfriend's in it?" I didn't wait for her to answer. I pulled Avery against me. Eric said I was supposed to touch her, so I was going to touch her. I had other reasons for wanting to, but I ignored them. I *also* forced myself to ignore the fact that my cock was lengthening and heading in her direction.

The girl snapped some selfies with us and then sniffed and walked away, as if we'd served our purpose. That was fine with me. I turned to Avery, not letting her go. I was very aware that her skin was hot to my touch. My vodka-befuddled brain started wondering if the heat was from her or from me, but I was getting too confused to think it through. I just knew I wanted to keep my arms around her. "Would you like to dance?"

She looked stricken. "Uh…yes?"

"Is that a yes that's actually a no?" I asked.

Avery composed her face and smiled at me bravely. "It's a yes. I'm not really a big dancer, though."

"Me either. It's not like there's a lot of room down there for my moves anyway. I can do a mean robot, but that's about the extent of my talent." I laced my fingers through hers and pulled her down the stairs.

Another server met us at the landing and offered us

more shots. "On the house, Mr. Layne," she said and winked. "Go Warriors!"

Avery and I each did another ill-advised shot, and then I pulled her into my arms on the dance floor. "For someone who's not a big drinker or a big dancer, you're sure managing nicely tonight," I said.

She put her arms around my neck, eighth-grade dance style. "I'm at your service, Mr. Layne. Remember?"

I leaned down to her ear. "I'm sorry I was a dick when you first showed up."

Even though that was the booze talking, I meant it. *A drunken man's words are a sober man's thoughts.* Cass, one of my "deep" football buddies, often said that. Usually when we were drunk and he was telling me how I could improve my game.

Avery trained her clear blue eyes on me. "S'okay. You've been through a lot lately."

I wanted to know what it was she'd been through, what her story was, but the loud, thumping base and the crowd of people around us weren't really the best place for a deep conversation. So I just wrapped my arms around her and pulled her to me. That same server showed up next to us with more shots. "Your buddy told me to keep 'em coming," she yelled and pointed at the mezzanine. Eric leaned over, smiling and giving us the thumbs up.

Avery looked at me nervously.

"One more for courage," I said, downing it. I needed courage tonight. My cock twitched again, trying to reach out and touch her. It'd been a long time, and at this stage of my buzz, I couldn't lie to myself. I was totally attracted to her. I ran my hands down her back. I was about to cross some lines, I could tell. My hard-on was getting thicker by the second.

Still, I wanted Avery to make her own choices. That was the only way I'd be able to live with myself.

I gestured toward the shot. "Don't drink that if you don't want to—don't do *anything* you don't want to do tonight."

Her eyes lit up. "Thank you for saying that," she said, sounding genuinely grateful. She eyed the small glass. "I guess I could use some more courage." She knocked back the shot, and I watched as she grimaced while it went down.

Then we grinned at each other like we were allies in a secret war.

I pulled her back to me, for better or for worse. This girl needed protection. And I wanted to keep seeing her eyes light up like that.

That'd been my last thought as ran my hands down her body, relishing the feel of her against me. *I want to be the one to light them up.*

And now I sat in my gym, feeling sick and shaky from my regular old hangover as well as a guilt hangover. I sighed and picked up even heavier weights, ignoring the vibrations of my phone. I wasn't trying to be a douchebag last night. I was *trying* to make Avery's eyes light up.

They said the road to hell was paved with good intentions. I had a sinking feeling I was about to find out if they were correct.

CHAPTER 9

AVERY

I stayed in my room the entire next day, venturing out only for a run to the kitchen for ibuprofen, water, and coffee—I still couldn't look at food. And I was petrified to face Chase. Elena called me on the loaner phone she'd packed. "Nice work, Avery. I'm loving these pictures of you and Chase out on the town. You guys look like you had a good time."

"We did." I swallowed hard. I'd taken the ibuprofen, but nothing had stopped the pounding in my head. I vowed to never touch hard alcohol again.

"How's he treating you?" the madam asked.

I forced myself to sit up and winced at how my whole body hurt. "He's very…nice. His agent wanted us to go out so we could be photographed. It seemed to go well."

"So, is this going to work out? I don't normally call my girls when they're on assignment, but this is a very special client. I wanted to be sure that you're comfortable, but also that you're confident Mr. Layne is satisfied with the service."

"Everything's going great." I felt a pit of dread form in my stomach. *Chase and I had sex last night, and he practically ran, screaming, out of my room this morning. I'm afraid to see him.* "Thank you so much for giving me this job, Elena. I'll never be able to say that enough."

I won't live long enough to say thank you appropriately— I'll probably die from embarrassment first. As soon as I face him again.

Elena clucked her tongue in approval. "I'm thrilled it's working out. Please get in touch if you need anything. I'll keep watching you online. I'm very pleased, Avery. Keep up the good work."

I plastered a smile onto my face even though she couldn't see me. "Thank you. I will. I promise."

I hung up and lay there, miserable and confused.

There was a knock on the door. I perked up, hoping it was Chase.

"Avery?" Eric called.

Even though I liked the agent, my face fell.

"Um…yeah?"

"Do you want some food?"

"God no," I said.

"Let me know if that changes. Listen, first thing tomorrow, we're meeting a broker to shop for condos in the Leather District. Photo opportunity," he called, sounding so chipper that I sunk back underneath my covers, away from the harsh brightness of his voice. "Just relax. I'll get you some ginger ale—so you don't puke like I just did."

I groaned. Eric was a seasoned professional in more ways than one. I had no idea how Chase was faring today—with his hangover or his guilt. Sighing, I got up and trudged to the shower. Even if I didn't feel good, I had to look good.

Just in case I had to face him.

CHASE

"I don't want to go real estate shopping, for fuck's sake," I said. I was holding a protein shake so tightly in my hands I almost crushed it.

"We're not going until tomorrow. Relax."

"I can't relax," I grunted. "I'm hungover, Eric. Really fucking hungover."

"So am I," Eric said, but his complexion looked too healthy for that to be true.

"Why don't you look as bad as I feel?" I asked suspiciously.

"Because I took painkillers last night. And I threw up this morning," Eric said smugly.

"Lucky." I sat down and winced. My muscles were sore from lifting, and my head was killing me.

"How about you?" Eric asked suspiciously. "You sleep okay?"

I had no intention of telling him that I'd slept with Avery. It had been a mistake—one that was never going to happen again—and it was none of his business. "If you call passing out sleeping, I guess so."

I yawned and felt Eric studying me. "What?" I snapped.

"Nothing." He shrugged. "Do you want to discuss the table dancing? Or the body shot? Or…anything else?"

I scrubbed my hands over my face. "There's nothing to discuss."

My agent smiled at me. "If you say so."

I headed to my room to take a shower. "You're seriously in too good of a mood to be around when I'm this hung. Ugh. Stay away from me."

"My pleasure," he called.

I grunted again and then headed down the hallway.

Avery popped out of her room, her hair soaking wet. She took one look at me, yelped, and jumped back inside her room, slamming the door.

I couldn't help it. Nasty headache aside, I laughed. And then knocked on her door. "Avery."

"Mm-hmm?" she answered, trying to sound casual from inside her room.

"Do you need something?"

"No," she said immediately, and I knew it was a lie.

"Why'd you come out here, then?" I wanted to help her, but more than that, I wanted to see her. I needed to know that she was okay.

She opened the door a crack and miserably peered out at me. "I just wanted another towel. I thought I had more in here, but I don't." She looked as if she were about to cry.

"I'll get you one," I said. "It'll just take a sec."

I hustled down to the linen closet and pulled out a stack of towels for her. Poor thing. She was in her room like a prisoner because I couldn't keep my dick out of her last night. I had to make this right.

She opened the door a little for me, and my heart melted when I saw her. Her long hair was wet, soaking her T-shirt, and she looked innocent, sexy, and beautiful without her makeup on. "Hey," I said. "I'll put these in the bathroom for you."

"You don't have to. I'll take them," she said, and it sounded as if she were struggling to keep her voice even.

I looked at her and sighed. "Can I...talk to you?"

She nodded, and even though she crossed her arms against her chest, she stepped aside so I could come in. Eric had put her in the guest suite, so she had her own sitting area, laundry, and a full bathroom. I set the towels down and took a quick scan of the room. The sheets were stripped from the bed, and I could hear the washer running. "About last night—" I started.

Avery shook her head. "I'm so sorry. I don't *ever* drink that much. And I've *never* had shots like that before. I don't know what got into me," she babbled, motioning to me. "I mean...I *know* what got into me— but I don't know *how* it got in there. I mean, I do. I mean, I don't. Oh God, please make me stop talking!" She cringed and put her face in her hands.

"It's okay," I said. I wanted to pull her into my arms and make her feel better, but I knew it would only make it worse. And for some strange reason—maybe being back in her room or the fact that she clearly had no bra on underneath that damp T-shirt—my dick was getting hard again. *Traitor.* Jesus Christ, I needed to get control of that thing.

"Listen. Avery." I reached out and squeezed her hands, which was as much contact as I could allow myself. "Last night is on *me*. I'm the one who took you drinking and convinced you to do those shots. I'm the one who asked you to dance and then started manhandling you. I'm really sorry."

She looked up at me. "You don't need to be sorry. You hired me as your date. You were doing what you were supposed to."

"And so were you," I said, trying to soothe her. "But I won't ask you to do that again. At least…not the last batch of stuff we did."

"Oh." She looked stricken. "Okay."

I squeezed her hands again, trying to reassure her. "Not because you did anything wrong or that I didn't like last night—of *course* I did."

A hot blush started to creep up her cheeks. "I asked you to come here to pretend to be my girlfriend in the public eye," I explained gently. "I didn't ask you to come here so I could take advantage of you."

Her face was a miserable shade of red. "But you didn't take advantage of me. I wanted to do…that last batch of stuff with you. I didn't do it because I thought I had to. Even though I *am* a hooker." Her chin wobbled almost imperceptibly.

"Don't cry," I said. "Fuck."

"I'm not." Her voice sounded thick with unshed tears.

"I guess I'm making this worse." I sighed. "Listen. I

want you to be here, and I wanted to be with you last night. But I don't want you to think that you're going to have to...*service* me like that for the rest of the time you're here. Because that's not who I am. Last night was a one-off."

"Got it." Her voice sounded neutral now, as if she'd wrangled it back under control. She dropped her hands from mine and grabbed a towel. "We're going out tomorrow, right?"

"Right." I searched her face. The blush was fading, and the chin wobble was no longer detectable.

She stopped on her way to the bathroom and turned back. "I don't have to go with you, you know. If you need some space."

"No—I want you to come," I said. "We're shopping for our new condo together, remember?" I grinned at her, trying to lighten the mood. "You sort of need to be there."

She plastered what was clearly a fake smile to her face and nodded. "Of course."

Avery disappeared behind the door, and I was left there, feeling as though I'd messed something important up very, very badly.

A playbook is what I need. A playbook for women.

They were definitely trickier than football.

CHAPTER 10

AVERY

The next morning I went through my clothes, selecting them carefully. Elena had packed some white jeans and a fitted, patterned coral tank top for me. I tried the outfit on and looked at my reflection in the mirror, pulling my hair over one shoulder.

I couldn't imagine having a closet filled with clothes like these. For being so hungover so recently, I looked much better than I should. Pretty even.

But still not good enough for Chase Layne.

I understood his position. He didn't want to take advantage of me, and a guy like Chase didn't have to pay for sex. I respected the fact that he didn't want me to… service him again. He was above that sort of conduct, and I admired him for it.

I blew out a sigh and regarded my eyes in the mirror. I was not going to let what happened between us send me into a spiral of self-hate. I was working as an escort because I needed the money. I'd had all sorts of honest jobs, and I hadn't been able to come close to getting ahead. I wasn't going to torture myself for wanting that.

Plus, I'd had *fun* with him. I couldn't remember the last time I'd relaxed and had fun. Maybe never.

And I'd loved the sex. I'd *definitely* never loved sex before.

But the fact was, it wasn't going to be like that with me and Chase. We were strictly for show.

You're only pretending to be in his league, I reminded myself.

So I was going to wear the nice clothes Elena had sent me, hold his hand and smile in public, and keep all of my other body parts to myself...even though they wanted him. Bad.

And if the thing that hurt the worst was my heart, there was no way in hell I was ever going to show it.

BEFORE I WENT out to meet them, my phone buzzed. It wasn't Elena's number this time.

My stomach dropped. That meant it had to be my sister.

"Lila?" I answered the phone, almost in a whisper.

"Is that you, Avery?" she practically screeched. "Are you *Chase Layne's* girlfriend now? Holy fucking *fuck*!"

"Wh-why are you calling me?" I asked. "I told you to only use this number if it's an emergency—"

"Because my baby sister's on the news!" she interrupted me, sounding much too excited. "I saw your pictures at the restaurant and at that club and I *had* to check in. So, how are you? More importantly, how the hell did you end up moving in with Chase Layne and being his insta-girlfriend? What is *up*, seriously?"

"I'm fine." But now that she'd called me, I was anything but. Lila never just 'checked in'. She found me when she needed something, which was usually in the form of some sort of bailout.

"So...are you actually, suddenly and out-of-the-blue, *dating* Chase Layne? Or is this one of your jobs?" she asked.

I bristled, not wanting to hear her say it out loud. I wished I'd never confided in my sister about Accommo-Dating. "It's none of your business, is what it is," I said stiffly.

"I just think it's funny—not funny ha-ha, but funny coincidental—that you finally managed to get ahead on our rent, say you're heading out of town, and the next day, I see you in the news with the Warriors quarterback. And you look as if you're madly in love with him!"

"He's really nice," I offered lamely.

She snorted. "The money, plus the fact that you never mentioned this guy before makes me...suspicious. That this isn't the real thing, you know?"

She was fishing. There was the bait, but I wasn't going to take it. I said nothing. I was too busy counting backward from one hundred so I didn't jump through the phone and throttle her.

"C'mon. You don't have to be shy with your own sister..."

"Do you want something, Lila?" I asked flatly. It wasn't really a question. Of course she wanted something.

"Well, he's a multi-millionaire. And if he's paying you enough to cover our rent, I was hoping there was something extra," she said innocently. "You know—so I don't starve."

"You could always get your own paycheck to ward off starvation," I offered.

"You don't have to be so high and mighty." Whenever I recommended that she work for a living, I was being *high and mighty*. "It's not as if you have a lot of room to feel superior to me."

I said nothing. *Let her starve.*

"Are you really going to be mean to me like this?" she asked, her voice a whine. "There's seriously nothing to eat."

"Fine," I mumbled in defeat. I didn't want to keep supporting my sister and her bad habits, but I couldn't say no to her. She always made me feel so guilty. I also didn't want her interfering with my life right now.

"Great." Her tone turned instantly brighter. "Can you do it sooner rather than later, though? Like today?"

I could feel a Lila headache coming on, which was actually worse than the vodka one I'd had yesterday. My sister seemed hell-bent on draining me financially and emotionally. "There's a safe in the kitchen, in the cabinet next to the microwave," I said. "Go get it. I'll give you the combination." There was a muffled pause as I heard her moving through our tiny apartment, locating the safe. I gave her the combination and I heard her sharp intake of breath as she counted the money inside.

"Shit," Lila said. "You've got two thousand dollars in here. You've been *hiding* this from me?"

"Not hiding," I said. *Protecting.* I'd put the money in there after Elena gave me the advance, just in case Lila came sniffing around, looking for a handout. "It's an emergency fund. It's all we've got."

Lila snorted, and I could picture her pocketing the

bills. "I betcha Chase Layne's got a lot more than this," she said. "But it'll do. For now." She would probably go out and buy weed, then buy herself an expensive new outfit and get her hair and nails done. She was beautiful, but she was vain, and she'd always had a taste for the finer things in life. Champagne taste on a *Boone's Farm* budget, just like my mother.

"Thanks, Ave. You always come through. See ya around," she said.

"Lila. Wait." I clenched my fist, not wanting to have to ask her for a favor, but not having a choice. "You can't mention this to anyone."

She laughed. "It's all over the Internet. It's not like you two are hiding it."

"Do we have an Internet connection, all of a sudden?" I asked.

Lila cleared her throat. "No, but my dealer does. He's the one who showed it to me. He recognized you."

My stomach fell. "Great. That's just perfect." My sister and her dealer were a little too close for both my comfort and her health. Once I got paid, I was moving her across town and away from him. "But listen—you can't tell anyone I'm your sister. Or about the escort service. You can't talk to *anyone* about this—not even your dealer. Not another word. I mean it." I could hear the pleading tone in my own voice.

She paused for a beat, probably calculating her options and how much they could earn her. "Why not?"

"Because it's a secret." I swallowed hard. *Fucking Lila.* I'd sacrificed so much to keep a roof over her head, and still, I couldn't trust her. There was only one person that Lila loved, and it wasn't me.

It was herself.

"If you do," I said, trying to stay calm, "I'll lose my job. I won't get paid. On top of that, I signed a confidentiality agreement. If that gets breached—by me or by you—they'll come after us for damages."

"Good luck collecting," she said.

"Still, it could ruin us." I desperately searched my brain for something that she cared about, something that I could lord over her. "This is a big deal. Chase Layne is a big deal. If we hurt him, we'll become local pariahs. It could get us banned from *everything*—shops, restaurants. Bars, even," I babbled. "Your dealer might even drop you." I crossed my fingers that the threat of any one of these things might be enough to convince my sister to keep her mouth shut.

"You really think I'm that dumb, Ave?" she asked, then paused for a beat. "Wait—are *you* actually that dumb? That I would believe..."

"Just stop it," I hissed at her. "The point is, if you mess this up for me, we lose. That I work for the agency and that Chase's people hired me has to stay confidential. If I finish the job, I'll get paid. A lot." I winced. This was going to come back and bite me later. I knew it.

"How much?" she asked.

"More than we have," I said.

"We don't have anything," she sniffed. "But listen. I'll make you a deal."

I groaned. She was always making deals. "What?"

"You get me enough money for some nice new clothes and a pocketbook—a nice one, not like that plastic thing I have from TJ Maxx—and pay for me to get my nails done, and my hair colored, and stuff like that, and I'll *think* about it. *Plus* the money you were hiding from me. Okay? Sound fair?"

"No, it doesn't sound fair," I said. I was turning fucking *tricks* to keep my sister off the streets, and she wanted a *pocketbook?*

I knew her. As if she was a child, she wanted the new and the shiny, and she wanted it *now*.

And if I didn't give it to her, she was going to throw a massive temper tantrum.

"Okay," I said, hating both myself and her. "Take that money for now. I'll send you more when I can."

"That's my baby sister coming to her senses," Lila cooed. "I'll be in touch. Soon. I have a feeling this assignment's gonna work out great for both of us. Chase

Layne's a fucking *goldmine*. Things are finally looking up. The sky's the limit now, Ave. I know it."

"Don't use this number again," I warned, my voice hoarse.

"Whatever." She hung up before I could try to reason with her.

I put the phone down and hung my head. *Lila doesn't want a pocketbook from TJ Maxx. Lila wants a nicer one. Lila wants a manicure. Lila wants, wants, wants...*

After a minute I sat up and pulled myself together. What *I* wanted right now was to pretend my sister didn't exist. The fact that she'd learned about my assignment didn't bode well for me. Or for Chase, for that matter, and his large piles of money...

I winced. He didn't deserve to be infected by my problems, by my poverty...by my sister. He was an innocent bystander who also happened to be the key to me never having to hook again. I vowed, right then and there, to keep him safe.

I just had to figure out how.

CHAPTER 11

CHASE

"You need to see this," Eric said, waking me up.

"Huh?" I said, groggy.

Eric held up his iPad. "It's Jess. She went public with Pax. She must've seen the pictures from the other night and flipped out."

He opened up her *Instagram* page and handed the tablet to me. There was picture after picture of Jess and Pax at some pool. Jess's silicon-enhanced assets were on full display, as was Pax's puffed-out chest. They were kissing in some of the pictures, their arms draped over each other. The taglines said "#reallove".

It looked as though I'd started a pissing contest with her, after all.

I put the iPad down and scrubbed my hands over my

face, yawning. "Wes isn't going to be happy, but otherwise, I couldn't give a fuck."

Eric was watching me thoughtfully. "I told you so."

"About which thing?"

"That hiring Avery was the right move." He sounded a little smug. "If you'd seen these pictures a week ago, you would've been a mess. Worried about what your teammates were going to say and how this was going to play out. But you're calm. I like you when you're calm."

"Gee, thanks."

He clapped me on the shoulder. "The point is, when you're calm that means you're in control. And that's what the Warriors need. Things are getting better, buddy. I told you so."

"You already told me that you told me so," I groaned, "so get out."

After he left, I couldn't go back to sleep. I sat on my bed, replaying the images from that night over and over in my head…again. What Eric said was true—I was calm about Jess and Pax's pictures, and this girl was the difference.

I just needed to figure out what that meant.

AVERY

"You look lovely," Chase said as I went out to meet him and Eric. He held out his big hand to me, smiling. *What a difference forty-eight hours, five quarts of alcohol and a little pokey-pokey made.* He was being positively civilized.

I was shaky from the conversation with my sister, but I tried to hide it as we headed out to an SUV waiting in the drive. The driver opened the door for us, and we piled in. "Kind of reminds me of the other night," Eric said. "Anybody want a drink?"

"No," Chase and I said at the same time.

Eric laughed. "You two. Cute." He gave me a quick, knowing glance that made me blush. Either Chase had told him that we'd spent the night together, or he'd seen enough at the club to guess.

"So," Eric said, turning to Chase. "We're looking at a couple of condos in the Leather District. Very trendy, modern, in up-and-coming buildings. I called the *Gazette* and a couple of the local sports blogs, so they know we're doing this. We should expect some coverage." He glanced through the back window, his glasses glinting in the sunlight. There was a line of cars pulling out after us, clogging the residential Wellesley street. "Looks like we already have some admirers."

Chase glanced out the window. "My neighbors must hate me."

"Your neighbors won't care, so long as you win the Super Bowl," Eric said. "So what we're looking for right now are two different things. First, we need to see if you actually want to live in one of these places. Second, we need to show you and Avery looking very much in love, like you're thrilled to be shopping for a home together. Are you two okay? Or are you still too hungover?"

"I'm fine," I said immediately. *It's been an interesting couple of days. I'd finally been gloriously, properly fucked by star quarterback Chase Layne, who now says I don't ever have to 'service' him again...and he's currently sitting next to me with all of his big muscles bulging in plain sight, just out of my reach, taunting me and my lady parts. And speaking of being fucked, I'm about to be royally, unscrupulously fucked over by my blackmailing sister. Because apparently she doesn't care if I have to suck cock in order to buy her a pocketbook. But I'm fine, Eric, really! Thank you so much for asking. You and your stupid purple shots and your shiny designer glasses and your smug lack of a hangover...*

"It's cool," Chase said, breaking my reverie. "but I think I'd also like to look at some of the Beacon Hill listings. Some of the more traditional stuff."

"But the Leather District is a hot market right now," Eric countered. "We're trying to show the public Chase Layne 2.0. A new and improved you with a trendy loft and a hot, new girlfriend."

"But *vintage* Chase doesn't want to live in a loft with exposed pipes. He likes classic," Chase said and laughed. "And he's paying for it, so he gets a say."

"Don't talk about yourself in the third person," Eric warned. "You know I hate it when you do that."

A grin spread over Chase's face. "Chase Layne wouldn't do that to you."

Eric shook his head. "Jesus Christ. You drive me *crazy*."

"Chase doesn't want to drive you crazy, but he *does* want to look at real estate in Beacon Hill," Chase said, continuing to taunt Eric.

"Um," I said, interrupting them, "I have a question." I decided to shove the errant, problematic thoughts from my head and focus on business.

"Please," Eric said, "anything to make him stop. Shoot."

"What's going to happen when I'm done working for you guys?" I blurted out, unable to keep the words from tumbling out. This issue had been bothering me since Elena told me about the assignment, but the long line of press cars following us and my sister's escalating set of demands made it seem more pertinent. I needed this to work so I could get paid and get out of this situation in one piece—and Chase did, too. "Isn't everyone going to know that this was all an act?"

Chase looked stymied, and Eric looked vaguely thoughtful. "We're still figuring out the exit strategy," he said.

"We are?" Chase asked. He shrugged. "I hate to admit it, but I was so worried about getting this whole thing started, I hadn't started worrying about how to end it."

Eric patted him on the arm. "We'll handle it when the time comes, buddy. You don't need to worry about it, either, okay Avery? We're just getting warmed up. Let's relax and enjoy the ride." He smiled knowingly at me. *Enjoy the ride, indeed.*

He turned back to Chase. "Your relationship will seem more natural if we don't plan the whole thing out. Like there's really something going on between you to." He gave his friend a long, probing look. "Unless of course, we don't need to worry about that because something *is* going on with you two..."

I felt myself start to blush, and Chase scowled at Eric. "Stop digging."

Eric held his hands up in mock defeat. "Whatever you say, Boss."

We drove through Chinatown into the sleek Leather District. Industrial and more traditional, brick buildings intermixed and soared, side-by-side, into the skyline. We pulled down Beach Street, past a wine bar and a high-tech office, and parked. "This is it," Eric said, hopping out and motioning to an impressive high-rise.

A handsome, well-dressed man waved toward us from down the street. The sun glinted off of his dark skin and accentuated the whiteness of his teeth when he smiled.

"Is that the broker?" Chase asked. "He dresses better than you, Eric."

"Can you stop talking now?" Eric asked, watching the broker. "That *is* a nice suit, though."

The man reached us and held out his hand to Chase. "I'm Jackson Pryce."

Chase grabbed his hand. "Chase Layne."

Jackson's polite smile turned into a grin. "I'm a huge fan. Are we looking good this year?"

"As soon as I get back out onto the field, we'll be looking a lot better." He motioned to me. "This is my girlfriend, Avery. And my agent, Eric Taylor."

"A pleasure," Jackson said. "Let's go take a look at this unit. It's top-of-the-line. Unless you want to wait for these gentlemen." He motioned toward the cars that were pulling up behind ours, cameramen spilling out of them.

"We can wait for a minute," Eric said. He positioned me next to Chase and smoothed both of our hair while he continued to talk to the broker. "What's the neighborhood like?"

"Very nice," Jackson said. "Upscale. It's a younger crowd that's moving in down here. They like the industrial style of the buildings."

"You got anything in Beacon Hill?" Chase asked him conspiratorially.

Jackson pointed at him. "I pegged you for a Beacon-Hill type. I have a classic townhouse. All the bells, whistles, and wainscoting you could hope for."

"That's sounds nice," Chase said. He turned to me. "Doesn't that sound nice, babe?"

I had no idea what sort of bells and whistles there would be, but I loved the Beacon Hill neighborhood, and I was somewhat stupidly thrilled that he'd just called me *babe*. "It does. But we should look at this one, too. I think Eric really wants to see it."

Eric shrugged a little defensively. "I like modern."

"Maybe you can finally buy a place up here so you don't always have to crash with me," Chase said. A few photographers had sidled up near us, and Chase casually threw his arm around me. "This is Jackson Pryce," he called pointing at the broker. "He's with Boston Premiere Realty. Best in the business. Now if you'll excuse us, Avery and I are looking for a new home." He squeezed me close, and we both smiled for the photographers. My worries about Lila lifted; the sun on my face and Chase's arm around me were like a balm.

We entered the lobby of the building. It was beautiful but austere with soaring windows and ultra-modern light fixtures. We went into the industrial-sized elevator, and as soon as the doors were closed, Chase turned to Jackson. "I can already tell this is not a good fit." He looked at Eric. "This is all you, buddy. You buy this one. I'll buy the Beacon Hill one."

"Sounds good to me," Jackson said, beaming.

Eric sighed and rolled his eyes. "Just give it a chance." We entered the massive space on the third floor, and I was impressed by the views of the district and the financial buildings beyond, and the exposed brick and the extremely high-end kitchen. Chase turned to me. "What do you think? Could you see yourself growing old with me here?"

For some reason, his words cut me. But I bravely plastered a smile on my face. "I like it, but it's not my style. But if you like it, that's all that matters."

Chase put his arm around me and turned to Jackson. "It's not for us. Sorry. Can we head over to the one on Beacon Hill?"

Jackson flashed us a brilliant smile. "I like to see two people on the same page. A lot of the couples I show places to want completely different things, and I always know it's going to end badly. But you two…"

Chase smiled at the broker and squeezed me against him protectively. "We're cute. We know. So…let's get out of here. Between the club the other night and this condo, I'm starting to feel old and out of place. Maybe a house with some history will do me good."

We left and drove to Charles Street, and I looked at the gorgeous homes with longing. The Beacon Hill neighborhood boasted classic Bostonian architecture, charming and grand. Pristine brick houses lined the streets, with classic shutters and window boxes filled with flowers. I could picture Chase living in this neighborhood with his beautiful wife and adorable children.

Chase let out a low whistle as we pulled up to the curb. He looked at a striking brick-faced home. "Now *this* is what I'm talking about. What do you think, Avery?"

I swallowed hard. "This is a gorgeous neighborhood." *I will never live anywhere like this.*

"I like it, too," Eric said. "I'd love to get you in a trendy loft, but even I can admit that this is more your style."

Jackson was waiting at the top of the granite steps. "Chase Layne, welcome home. You and Avery go ahead and take a walk through the house. I think you're going to love it, but I want you to see for yourselves. I'll be waiting for you out here. Come find me when you're done."

"I only have one question," Chase said. "How much is this going to cost me?"

Jackson beamed at him. "Eight-point-five million."

Chase opened his mouth, closed it, then smiled tightly. "I don't know if my ex is going to leave me with that much, but we'll go take a look." He reached out and grabbed my hand, leading me through the door. We entered the massive foyer, which had black and white floors, a stunning staircase and an enormous crystal chandelier. "This is a little formal, don't you think?"

I nodded. "But if you lived here, you'd make it homey. There would be sneakers and football pads everywhere. And beer. Much less stiff."

"I can picture the sneakers." His eyes sparkled at the inner vision. "And the beer." He kept his hand clamped over mine as we went through the rest of the house. Chase seemed enamored by the architectural details of the home.

"Look at these," he said, examining the light fixtures in one of the halls. "I can't tell if these are original or not, but they match the house so well." He turned to me. "Do you like this kind of stuff? Or do you just think I'm crazy?"

"I do like this kind of stuff," I said. "But you're awfully excited about the light fixtures." He grinned at me, and I couldn't help but grin back. I hadn't imagined that the big, sexy quarterback was an architecture nerd.

"When I bought the house in Wellesley, it was for convenience. It was an easy drive to the stadium." He shrugged. "I mean, I *liked* it, but it wasn't a big deal. And then Jessica decorated it, and I didn't like it as much anymore." He examined some floor-to-ceiling built-in bookcases before turning to me. "She posted some pictures of her and Pax on social media today. They were hanging all over each other."

"Oh... Chase, I'm sorry."

"She's probably pissed about our pics from the other night." He shook his head. "I'm fine with it. Their relationship was going to come out sooner or later."

"Are you worried about the team?" Eric had explained further why they'd hired me. Chase was worried about how his wife's transgressions were going to impact the Warriors.

"Everybody keeps texting me about how hot you are." He pulled out his phone and scrolled through it. "I haven't read all these new messages, but it looks like they're saying the same thing. That Pax is a douche."

"So, that's good," I offered. *Except for the part where your wife's sleeping with your teammate and posting it all over social media. And the fact that you're going back to prac-tice with him in a couple of days.*

"Hiring you is working out better than I thought." His face reddened when he realized that there was a double meaning there. "Seems like we're making the best of a bad situation," he coughed.

"Good," I said, trying to soothe him. "I'll be so happy if I can actually help."

Chase coughed again, still red, and turned back to the bookcase. "I've always wanted a house like this. It would be a dream come true."

We went into the kitchen, and he inspected each item, finally stopping at the refrigerator. "This is the biggest refrigerator I've ever seen. I think this could be the house for me." He looked at me. "By the way, Avery, can you cook?"

I nodded. "Nothing too fancy, but I can make the basics. I did all the cooking in my house growing up." I decided not to mention why that was, or that for the last three years, my diet had consisted largely of Ramen noodles, fast-food cheeseburgers and crackers stolen from the *Sizzling Ranch.*

"Can you make lasagna?" he asked hopefully.

I smiled at him. "I can make a pretty mean lasagna."

"That's awesome. I've been eating nothing but take-out…" His voice trailed off longingly.

"I'll make it for you."

"Soon?" His eyes glittered with excitement.

I laughed. He was a big, tough quarterback, but he was really being a baby about a lasagna. "Sure."

We continued with our tour of the home. We went up the grand staircase, and a chill went through me. I could picture kids playing up here, looking through the rails down at their parents. Each bedroom we entered was sunny and perfect. *What would it be like to live in a house like this?*

I was never going to find out, and I knew it. This was a different world from mine. A mere fifty-thousand dollars—more money than I'd ever had in my whole life—wasn't going to bridge the gap.

We went outside and found Jackson and Eric seated on the steps, enjoying the sun. "We'll take it," Chase told them.

We'll take it. I shivered. Chase sure was good at putting on a show.

Jackson clapped him on the back. "I *knew* this was the beginning of a beautiful friendship."

CHAPTER 12

CHASE

Jackson and I settled on a preliminary offer. He said he'd get back to me soon, and if everything went smoothly, we could probably close in a few weeks.

Things were moving fast, but that was fine by me. Onward and upward.

Eric paced down the sidewalk nearby, on a call with a client. I looked at the sun glinting off Avery's hair as she peered around the neighborhood. "It's such a great day," I said. "Do you want to go to the park?"

She turned to me and smiled. Which for some reason felt like she was punching me in the gut—in a good way, if that was possible. "Sure. That sounds nice."

"Then right this way, milady."

I jerked my chin at Eric. "We're walking. Take the car if you want. Catch you later."

He gave me the thumbs up and kept pacing.

One of the great things about this neighborhood was that it bordered the Common, which was the main park in Boston. It was filled with flowering trees and kids running around. The Common was centrally located in the city, close to Newbury Street's shops, restaurants and hotels, as well as the State House and the Freedom Trail. People didn't know it, but Boston was a walkable city. I'd be able to get to about a thousand restaurants from my new house, including my favorites in the North End.

The press had come, taken some pictures, and gone. Civilians might be snapping pics of us on their cellphones, and that was fine. I laced my fingers through Avery's as we walked to the park. Eric had mentioned that there were new pictures of us being posted, but I didn't want to think about that now. I wanted to enjoy the sun. My limbs felt loose and relaxed.

It was because I'd finally gotten laid. And because it had been awesome.

"It's so beautiful," Avery said, taking in the purple, flowering trees. "I never come here."

"Me either. But that's going to change." I spotted

something I'd forgotten about: the Swan Boats. "Do you want to take a ride?"

She looked surprised. "On the Swan Boats? I never have."

I squeezed her hand. "Let's do it. They don't do much —they just go back and forth, real slow."

"Perfect," she said.

We waited in line. A mom with two boys was in front of us. She kept trying to get them to stop staring. "Give them some privacy," she hissed.

One of them, who was probably eight, kept looking at me with big eyes.

"It's okay. I love kids," I told the mom.

"That's awfully nice of you." She beamed at me and turned to her son. "You can say 'hi'."

"Hi." The kid whipped off his baseball hat and held it out to me. "Will you sign my hat?"

"'Course, buddy," I said. "What's your name?"

"Tyler," he said, still staring at me. His eyes were huge in his face. "You're really big in real life, you know that? I have a lot of football cards and I watch all the games— and NFL Network—but I can't believe you're so *big*."

Avery smiled at the boy. "He eats a *lot*."

I smiled and handed him back his hat. "It's true. I do."

Tyler nodded. "I do, too."

"Do you drink milk?" I asked.

He nodded solemnly. "I love milk."

"I love milk, too. You wanna take a picture?"

"Yes." A huge smile broke out over his face. He came over, pulling his younger brother next to him and their mom snapped pictures, grinning the whole time. "This is so awesome," Tyler said. "This is the coolest thing that's ever happened to me."

"This is cool for me too, buddy. Thank you for making my day."

The mom leaned over to us. "You're very kind," she said. "Both my boys worship you. I love that you're a nice person in real life. Thank you again."

"It's my pleasure." I meant it.

I felt like I was on a high as Avery and I climbed onto our swan boat, which was a glorified pontoon boat decorated with large swans on the front. The sun dappled the water as the boat meandered around the park.

"This is fun," Avery said. She sounded a little shocked.

"You didn't think you'd like the *swan boats*? Everybody likes the swan boats."

She shook her head. "No. I meant being with you."

"You didn't think you'd like *me*? Everybody likes me." I pretended to pout.

"You weren't exactly nice when I showed up," she pointed out.

That humbled me. "I know. I'm sorry. But I wasn't expecting to like you, either."

"S'okay. We're making the best of it."

I grinned at her and squeezed her hand. "We sort of are, aren't we?"

"ARE you buying this house for you, or are you buying this house for Avery? Or to shove it in Jessica's face?" Eric asked me. "Not that there's anything wrong with that—the last option, anyway." We were sitting on my back deck, each of us nursing a Bloody Mary. My agent was studying my face again, searching for clues about my emotional state and annoying me.

I took a sip of my drink and scoffed at him. "I'm not buying a house for Avery. That might be the stupidest thing you've ever said, and that's really saying something."

Eric regarded me calmly. "I know you slept with her. I won't ask you for details, although I'm sure it was awesome. Otherwise, you wouldn't have been mooning over her all day, holding her hand and asking her if she got off on the wainscoting as much as you did."

"Why're you being a dick, Eric?"

"I'm not. I'm protecting you. Which is my job, if you'll remember." He sighed. "I wanted you to have fun the other night, and I'm glad you did. She's a nice girl, Chase. But she *is* also an escort."

"What are you really saying?" I asked.

He shrugged and looked out of the pool. "I want you to have fun, and I want you to be nice to this girl—but you can't run the risk of actually falling for her."

"There's no risk." I looked at my friend, my brow furrowed.

"We both know there's no future there," Eric said calmly. "That's all I'm saying."

I grunted in exasperation. "First, you yell at me for being a dick to her. Then you lecture me because you think I'm being too nice. Which is it?"

"It's neither. But I saw the look on your face today." He pursed his lips. "I know that Jessica wasn't the right person for you. And I would like my best friend to be happy at some point."

"Then let me figure out what that means for myself."

"I'm just looking out for you, buddy. I know you—and I don't want to see you get hurt again," he said.

"Chase Layne's a big boy. He can take care of himself."

He groaned. "For the love of God, stop talking about yourself in the third person."

"Eric?" I asked, changing gears. "You think that maybe you want to buy that loft in the Leather District?"

Eric looked surprised. "I don't think I need a place up here. I can always crash with you."

"That's actually something I wanted to talk to you about..."

ERIC MOVED out a few days later. Jackson Pryce was able to convince the sellers of the loft that a short-term rental was in their best interests given the current market conditions. I was pretty sure he was doing me a favor, but as I was buying an eight-point-five-million-dollar home from him, he sort of owed me.

Eric slapped me on the back as he was leaving. "I'm staying up here for the next couple of months," he said. "I can work remotely for my other clients, and *you* are my top priority right now. Anytime you want to go out, or need a photo opportunity or press conference, just call me."

He leaned in closer. "Are you kicking me out so you can play house with Avery?"

I patted him on the back. "You know you're welcome back anytime, brother. Just no shots."

"A Kick in the Crotch seemed like it served its purpose. It certainly worked out all right for you," Eric said, training his eyes on me. "And you still didn't answer my question."

I smiled at him tightly. "No, I did not."

Avery came out and hugged Eric. "Bye," she said, looking sorry to see him go. "Are you sure you're going to be okay without us? What're you going to do without anyone to bully into binge-drinking?"

"I'll think of something." Eric smiled at both us. "I feel like I'm a parent about to go on vacation and leave my teenagers at home."

I shook my head and noticed that Avery was blushing. My dick hardened at the thought of being alone in the house with her. *Down boy.* Jesus, that thing was going to get me in trouble.

But that wouldn't be the worst thing…would it?

CHAPTER 13

AVERY

It may have been mean, but when Chase asked me to go swimming the next day, I chose the sexiest bikini I had. It was black with strings and that was pretty much all there was to it. I looked at myself in the mirror, approving of how I looked even though I didn't approve of my motivations.

He'd asked Eric to leave for a reason. Seeing as I couldn't stop thinking about the other night, I was curious to find out what it was.

I threw on a cover-up and headed out back. It was a gorgeous day, warm without the typical New England humidity. Chase was already in the water, his massive shoulders bobbing in the aqua pool. I took a deep breath as I checked out his muscles. Good Lord, this man was turning me into one of Pavlov's dogs. I was looking at his naked chest and salivating.

No good could come of this.

"Avery, grab two beers." Chase grinned at me from the pool. "It's the nicest day ever. The water feels great." I went to the outdoor fridge and grabbed two IPAs. I brought them over and handed him one, threw off my cover-up, and proceeded to jump into the pool.

Chase's grin had turned appreciative. "You look pretty good in that suit. Did you put that on for me?"

Electricity crackled through me, but I just shrugged and stayed on my side of the pool. "I wear what they packed for me." A silence fell between us. *Great. Way to mention the escort service and kill the mood, Avery.*

"You haven't told me much about yourself," he said. He grabbed a floatie and hung onto it as he took a swig of beer. "It doesn't seem fair—you know I love old houses, football and beer. And you know about my ex and my douchebag of a cornerback. But what about you?"

"Oh. Huh. There's really not that much to tell…" I decided this was a good time to go underwater. Maybe if I stayed there long enough, he would forget what he'd asked me.

I came up for air and he was still there, floating calmly. "Are you avoiding the question?" He swam over to the side, grabbed the other beer, and handed it to me. "Drink. Drink some more. Then speak."

I sighed and did as I was told. The man was a quarterback. He wanted me to follow the play, and he wasn't taking no for an answer.

Omaha. Tell me about your life. Two, four, six, hike!

"I'm originally from Rhode Island. My sister and I live in Somerville now. I'm a waitress at a lovely buffet-style dining establishment, the *Sizzling Ranch*. You ever heard of it?"

Chase grinned at me. "I'm a big fan of their wings."

"No you are not," I said.

"Oh yeah. I am. And their buffalo dip."

"I manage the dip—I fill all those containers," I said, mock proud.

"That's hot," Chase said, flirtatiously, and took a sip of beer. He floated closer and a little thrill went through me. *So many muscles.* I watched as water beaded on his massive chest and ran down his pecs in rivulets. He looked like a Greek god.

And he was looking at me as if I were a mere mortal...that he was about to plunder.

"You know, I've been thinking..." he said.

I shivered. "About what?"

"About... Food."

I felt deflated but I laughed. "You want that lasagna, don't you?"

"Will you *please* make it for me tonight? I can have my service pick up any ingredients you need. Just make a list, babe."

Babe. I loved it when he called me that. "Of course I will." Like I could say no to those pecs or those big blue eyes.

"You're the best. I mean it." He floated closer and I held my breath. I really wanted to give him something more than just lasagna.

"There's something else I'm thinking about." His eyes locked with mine. "And that's you and what we did the other night. I can't stop. And that bikini's not helping."

I smiled at him, but my heart was beating wildly in my chest, and a fluttering, nervous little bird of hope rattling around in there.

"What I said before...after we, *you know*... About not wanting you to service me...that was true. I meant it." He came closer and I noticed I was shaking, probably from restraining myself. I wanted to feel those muscles. I wanted those lips on mine, and I wanted to trace the scruff that was growing in on his handsome face.

But I wasn't in charge here.

"I don't want to do anything that's going to hurt you," he said softly. He was close enough for me to touch him, but I didn't dare. "I don't want to take advantage of you, babe. I couldn't live with myself."

I swallowed hard. "What *do* you want?" I asked.

His eyes burned into mine. "I want to service *you*. I want to make you come again. I want you to scream my name, like you did before." He searched my face. "But I feel like I'm being selfish."

"That doesn't sound selfish to me at all," I blurted out.

Chase laughed, his eyes twinkling, the tension subsiding between us a little. "Do you know what I mean, though? You're here because I'm paying you. But I don't want you to feel like you have to be with me like *that*. Like it's part of your job." He swallowed, and I could see the muscles in his throat work. "I wouldn't feel right about it."

I nodded. "I know. I respect that."

He threw up his hands. "So what am I going to do with you?"

Make me scream your name again? Please?

I smiled at him. "I'm sure you can think of something." I never, ever let myself indulge. Not in anything. I left that to Lila—the clothes she pined for, the booze, the weed. I couldn't even remember the last time that I actually *wanted* something. I was too busy worrying all the time.

But I wanted Chase. I looked at him floating in the

water nearby, his hulking shoulders and killer body contrasting with his kind eyes. I wanted to kiss him, to feel his hands all over me. I wanted him inside me again. I wanted it *bad*.

And for once—even though it was for just right now —I was going to let myself have something. Something perfect.

CHASE

On those *Viagra* commercials, they say that if you have an erection for more than four hours, you need to call your doctor.

I was going on days. And I was pretty sure if I called the team doc and told him about it, he'd laugh at me and tell me to go jerk off.

But I had. Multiple times. And here I was, tenting my swim trunks.

I'm sure you can think of something, Avery said. All I'd been doing was thinking of all sorts of things, all of which involved her in different positions, some of which imaginarily had taken place in my pool.

Because…pool sex. Enough said.

So here we were. Game time. Avery came over and put her hands on my floatie, looking up at me. I noticed her pupils were dilated. "I can probably come up with something if you can't," she said.

And then she put her lips against mine, kissing me tentatively.

I groaned in pleasure as I kissed her back, my tongue seeking hers. *If she started it, maybe it's really okay...*

But I pulled back. "Avery—"

"You're not taking advantage of me," she said breathlessly. "Probably the opposite's true. But I can live with that if you can. Can you live with it?"

"Totally," I said at once.

"Good." She nodded. "Now, no more talking."

"Okay. And I can live with no more talking—until you scream my name," I said, pulling her back to me. I'd already waited for this too long. I ran my arms down her sides and she shivered. I crushed my lips against hers. She moaned as our tongues connected. I put my arm around her waist and kicked over to the shallow end, so I could concentrate on her body without both of us drowning.

She ran her hands over my face, softly exploring the beard that was growing in. She rubbed her tits against me as I deepened the kiss. I groaned, forcing my cock against her. She responded, brushing up against it, raking her hands down my back.

Oh fuck. I've been waiting for this.

My heart was hammering in my chest as I lifted her up by her ass and secured her legs around my hips. I headed for the stairs. I placed her gently on the side of the pool. She never broke the kiss and she kept her legs wrapped around me, drawing me against her. I undid her bikini top and tossed it to the side, pulling back long enough to see her in the sunlight. Her long blond hair hung over her shoulders, the golden strands glinting in the sunlight. Her blue eyes gazed up at me from underneath long lashes.

She was so pretty it hurt. "You're fucking gorgeous, babe," I said. I was breathing as hard as if I'd been doing wind sprints.

She smiled at me, clearly delighted, before pulling me back in for a sweet kiss that deepened with longing. I rubbed her nipples, which were hard and elongated, rising out of her perfectly round, luscious tits. I leaned down and took one bud in my mouth, sucking it until she moaned and arched her back. I flexed my hips and thrust my cock against her bikini bottom then, and we both sucked in a breath. I had to be inside her.

I pulled off her bottoms and parted her legs a little, looking at her naked sex in the sunlight, reveling in it. I leaned down and kissed the insides of her thighs, working my way over to her clit. She was already wet for me, and it wasn't just from the pool. I could tell. She cried out as I lapped at her, her muscles clenching. I tentatively stuck a finger inside her, then two, making sure she was ready for me. Her hips bucked as she tried to get my fingers to fuck her. *She was ready all right.*

I took her clit in my mouth and she cried out. That was it—I couldn't take it anymore. I pulled my bathing suit off and fisted my cock, looking at Avery as she sat there, visibly panting. And then she stood up, turned, and bent over the side of the pool, ass positioned right over the edge, legs spread apart, her sex glistening with moisture, ready for me.

Holy fucking fuck. That was so hot. She really might be the perfect woman.

I rubbed my cock against her slit, causing shockwaves to go through my body as I lubricated myself with her wetness. Then notched the tip against her opening. I inched myself into her slowly, feeling her body stretch to accommodate my girth.

I might be a cocky son-of-a-bitch, but I had an objectively huge dick.

She cried out in pleasure as I filled her, but I took it slow. I wanted to savor the feeling of being inside her. *So fucking tight.* I tentatively flexed my hips and she looked back over her shoulder at me. "Oh *fuck*, Chase," she said. "That feels so good."

That was all the encouragement I needed. I couldn't

stop myself from thrusting into her then, over and over. She cried out every time, her body vibrating and rocking against me in pleasure. I was in deep. My balls were heavy, slapping against her.

Oh fuck. Oh fuck, please don't let me come first—

"Chase!" she screamed, loud. She shattered around me, her whole body shaking, and that was all it took to push me over the edge. I came in her, hard, gripping her hips and spending myself into her. *Holy fuck.*

Our bodies rocked together, shaking in the last throes of our orgasms.

I lay down next to her, careful not to put my weight on her. She looked at me and grinned, looking happy and dazed.

"I knew you'd think of something," she said.

CHAPTER 14

AVERY

After that, of *course* I made him lasagna. I prepared a list and Chase had his mysterious service, whatever that was, go to Whole Foods and then deliver everything. I stayed in the kitchen the rest of the afternoon, happily chopping vegetables and making sauce. Chase hit the gym, caught up on some emails about endorsement stuff and then came to hang out with me.

He poured us each a glass of red wine and then sat down at the island, watching me cut a loaf of Italian bread in half and started spreading butter on it. "I could get used to this, you know. A beautiful woman making me dinner? I like it," he said.

"Jess didn't cook for you?" I asked.

He snorted. "*Hell* no. Actually, the last year we were together, I think she pretty much stopped eating."

"Why?" I couldn't imagine not eating on purpose.

"Because she was worried about getting fat. And bitches be crazy," he said. He looked up at me. "Present company excluded, of course."

"Oh, of course." *I'm just your escort, who you said you didn't want to sleep with, that keeps making you sleep with her. Not crazy at all.*

"What's she like?" I asked, curiosity getting the better of me. "Besides crazy?"

He shrugged. I noticed he'd gotten some sun today; his burnished, copper-color skin look like it was lit from within. "She was a pain in the ass. As soon as we got married, she showed her true colors. She's only out for herself."

"Ugh. I'm sorry." I sprinkled some mozzarella on the bread and Chase watched me with interest. "But why did you..." I wasn't sure how to phrase the next part without being too insulting or invasive. *Why did you stay with her? Why did you wait for her to leave you?*

"Stay married?" he asked. His eyes flicked down to his wine. "It's embarrassing."

"You can tell me," I offered. "It's not like we really need to keep secrets from each other. You know I'm a hooker and I know you were desperate enough to hire a hooker."

He laughed and shook his head. "When you put it that way... I guess I can speak freely."

"I think so," I said. "But you don't have to tell me if you don't want to."

His eyes met mine. "I didn't leave Jess because I didn't want to deal with it. I just wanted to get through this season. That's all I wanted to focus on. Not personal shit."

I nodded. "I get it."

He looked mildly surprised. "You do?"

"Sure." I put the bread into the oven and turned it onto broil. Chase's fancy oven had seemed like an alien spaceship to me at first, but I'd managed to figure it out. "You're the best quarterback in the NFL. *Ever.* I can't imagine you can get to a level like that without pushing almost everything else to the side. And your wife turned out to be someone different than you thought. Can't blame you for that —she's the one who was pretending. It's not like you can anticipate that someone's gonna let you down like that."

A deep V had formed on his forehead as he listened to me. "Huh."

I cringed, worrying that I'd either said too much or

just said the wrong thing. I busied myself tossing the salad. "Is that an annoyed 'huh' or...a good 'huh'?"

"It's a good 'huh'," Chase said. "I think you might be on to something. For a long time, I thought I deserved what I was getting with Jess. Because I'd misread her."

"Sort of like a penalty?" I asked.

He nodded. "Exactly. I messed up and I was paying for it."

"You misjudged her," I said. "I don't think it's worth beating yourself up over. You've been penalized. Resume regular play."

"Football talk, huh? Are you trying to charm me?"

I shrugged. "Only if I'm actually doing it right."

"It was close enough that I understood." He inspected his wine for a moment.

"You seem okay about her being gone," I ventured, "and mostly okay about her being with Pax. Aside from the nuisance factor."

"He got to me at practice. I shouldn't have gone after him like that, but he pushed my buttons hard." Chase scrubbed his hands across his face. "But since then, it's just been a couple of nasty texts from Jess and those selfies on Instagram. That's not worth freaking out over. But we'll see what they pull next. Jess usually has plans."

I nodded. "But at least you're out in front of it. I'm sure she doesn't like that one bit—that you've been photographed out and about, and that you're getting more attention." I'd read the news online; the sports community was largely condemning Jess and Pax, but they seemed to be enjoying Chase's post-split lifestyle. The mom we'd met at the swan boats had made the nicest Facebook post about meeting us and posted an adorable picture of Chase with the boys; it'd been shared about ten thousand times.

"I'm sure it's driving her crazy. Which is fine by me." He looked hopefully at the oven. "Is dinner almost ready?"

"It'll just be a minute," I said, checking the bread.

"So...enough about me. Tell me something else about you. Tell me more about your sister."

"There's not that much to tell." I groaned inwardly. I would much rather discuss Chase's ex than my sister. "She's older than me. Her name's Lila."

"What does she do?" Chase asked. He sounded genuinely curious.

"Um...her last job was at Jamba Juice. It didn't really work out."

"Why's that?" he asked.

"She...she's just not great at being responsible," I finally admitted. I wanted to be as honest with him as I could without getting into too much gory detail.

"So she's not working?"

I didn't look at him. I just shook my head. "Not right now." *She's off spending my emergency fund on weed and high-end cosmetics.*

"You said she lives with you. Do you...take *care* of her? Pay for everything?" Chase didn't seem to want to let this go.

I shrugged. "Just till she gets back on her feet."

"Is that why you're working for the service? I'm guessing you're not making a fortune at the good old *Sizzling Ranch*..."

I swallowed over a lump in my throat and just nodded. I was worried I wouldn't be able to get any words out.

"What about your parents?"

I shrugged again. "My mom died my senior year of high school. My dad...I don't know my dad." When I laid it all out like that, it sounded so...bleak.

"Aw, I'm sorry," he said. "What happened to your mom?"

"I just told you. She died." *She overdosed my senior year. I found her after school.*

What on Earth would he think of me if I told him *that*? And if I told him my unemployed, scheming sister was trying to blackmail me just so she could get a new pocketbook?

He'd probably run away, screaming. I wouldn't even blame him.

He held up his hands. "I'm not trying to make you upset. I just want to get to know you better. And we don't need to keep secrets from each other, like you said."

I nodded. "I know. But my family's not exactly fun to talk about. And my mom...she died of cancer." The lie tasted bitter and coppery, like battery acid on my tongue.

"I'm so sorry." He got up and came around the island, pulling me into his arms. "And just so you know, you don't have to tell me anything you don't want to. But if you decide you want to talk, I'm not gonna judge. I'm not like that, okay?" He kissed the top of my head.

Of course you're not. You're perfect. And this is just another example of what I'm going to be missing out on, once this assignment's over.

"Okay," I said, nodding against his chest, relaxing in spite of myself against his wall of well-meaning muscle. "Are you ready to eat?"

He took a step back. "Absofuckinglutely," he said. "It smells so good."

I shrugged self-consciously. "I hope you like it..."

CHASE

"Christ, woman, I have to unbutton my shorts," I said, rubbing my stomach. "That was amazing."

Avery looked at me with one eyebrow raised. "I can't believe you ate the entire pan of lasagna."

"You had some," I said defensively.

"I had one *piece*."

"I told you I've only been eating takeout. I needed some home-cooking."

She laughed and got up to clear the dishes.

"You can just leave those in the sink. Housekeeping will clean it up. That's one of the perks of being an NFL player. You don't have to do dishes."

"That's a pretty nice perk," Avery said.

I watched her as she ran the water in the sink. She was wearing one of my T-shirts, her hair up in a messy bun. Even though the rest of me was too stuffed to move, my cock twitched. *Shit.* I had to go back to practice soon. The day after tomorrow. Even though that'd been all I wanted, *now* all I wanted was to stay home on house arrest with Avery. "Do you want to watch a movie with me?"

Avery bit her lip. "I don't know, maybe..."

"C'mon. What are you worried about? I thought we already *did* all the things either of us could be worried about."

She shook her head. "I'm just worried that you...like really bad movies."

I grinned at her. "Trust me, I have great taste." I stood up and held out my hand for her, and she tentatively took it. "Let's see what I've got in my Netflix library."

I brought her into my bedroom, threw off my shorts and jumped onto the bed in just my underwear. She'd seen all of me, so I figured she could handle my boxer briefs. I grabbed the clicker as she sat down beside me. "Do you want to watch *Notting Hill* or something? Because I can do that—even though Hugh Grant makes me wanna barf. But I'm man enough to watch it with you."

She laughed. "I *do* love Julia Roberts, but I won't force her and Hugh on you. Is there some way we can meet in the middle?"

I scrolled through the offerings. "Have you watched *Game of Thrones*? I haven't had the time to sit down and start."

"I really don't watch that much TV," she said. "But I've heard *Game of Thrones* is awesome."

"You want to try it?"

"Okay." She grinned at me. "I'm game if you are. Get it? *Game.* That's a pun!"

"Wow," I said, flicking to the show and shaking my

head. For such a hot girl, she was surprisingly normal. And she told surprisingly bad jokes. "Just...wow."

AVERY

Three episodes later, Chase turned to me blearily. "I want to watch more, but I have to sleep."

"I really don't want you to turn it off, but do it. Otherwise, we'll be up all night!"

Chase laughed. "I know, right? Makes you want to grab a sword and go fight somebody."

"I love all the characters. I don't want anything bad to happen to them." I turned to him, rolling over on the pillow. "You don't think something bad's going to happen to them, do you?"

Chase grinned at me. "Nah. It's TV, right? There's gotta be a happy ending."

I frowned. "I don't know. I sort of have a bad feeling about it. " I sat up. "I better get going to bed. See you tomorrow, okay?"

Chase's face fell a little. "You don't want to stay? I'll let you sleep. I promise."

"Chase..." Of course I wanted to stay. What I didn't want to do was dig myself into an emotional hole I'd never be able to claw my way out of.

His big hand patted the bed. "I like having you here with me."

I liked being here with him, too. That was the problem.

He looked at me, pleading. "C'mon, just stay. Stay and snuggle with Chase."

I laughed. "You're a goof. But okay." I lay back on the bed, feeling way too comfortable as he wrapped his arms around me and pulled me against his chest. "Okay."

CHAPTER 15

CHASE

I woke up with my arm thrown over her, sunlight streaming into the room, like it was the most normal thing in the world.

I watched her as she slept. Her long blond hair tangled behind her, and her chest rose rhythmically and peacefully. Her face was smooth, calm. I wanted to reach out and touch her, but I should let her rest.

I couldn't remember the last time I'd hung out with a girl, gone swimming, had dinner, watched TV—and just had fun. I wasn't putting on any airs for Avery. Not because I didn't feel like I had to, given her situation, but because she was a *real* girl. She was pretty and sweet and awesome. She made me feel normal, like being myself was good enough.

Plus, she liked *Game of Thrones*. We were going to watch it again tonight.

I sighed and looked up at the ceiling, putting my hands behind my head. This was becoming a problem. I was asking Avery to make me dinner, sleep in my bed and to binge-watch Netflix with me—and she was my escort. And I'd sworn to myself—up-and-down—that I was not going to get involved with my escort.

Because I couldn't.

Oh yeah—and I'd fucked her. Twice. I'd fucked her *well*. It felt like her tight little body was made for mine.

She was waking up. She rolled over and looked at me, a happy smile breaking out over her face. "Hey."

I beamed back at her. "Hey yourself."

She stretched and her boobs jiggled beneath the filmy fabric of her T-shirt. *Speaking of that tight little body...* I leaned over and kissed her forehead, and then I pulled her against me.

Because I couldn't fucking help myself.

WE HAD SEX ALL DAY. In my bed. In my pool. On my patio. In my shower.

When housekeeping came, I locked us in my room and we both tried to tone down the screaming.

Every time we were done, I wanted her again. I was getting sore and raw.

Like I gave a fuck. I hadn't had sex like this in *years*. Ever, maybe.

And she made me breakfast. And lunch. And then we watched three more episodes of *Game of Thrones* and held hands the whole time.

Best. Day. Ever.

I hadn't even noticed my phone blowing up. When I finally checked it, there were a dozen texts and five missed calls from Eric.

I called him immediately, before he sent a SWAT team over.

"Hey buddy," I said.

"What the fuck, Chase? Since when don't you answer my texts?"

"Since I was working out all day," I lied.

"Bullshit," Eric said. "You were fucking Avery all day and I know it." He sighed. "Do you remember that the Children's Hospital fundraiser's tonight? You have to be there. Everybody's going to be there, including Wes and Tim."

"Of course I remember," I lied again. "We're going. It's at the Aquarium, right?"

"Yes. Listen, I'm pretty sure Pax and Jessica will be there, too," Eric warned. "So be prepared. I'll see you later, okay? We'll talk tonight."

"Yes sir."

I hung up and waited for Avery, who was in the shower. She came out, wrapped in a towel, and I immediately got hard again. My Johnson was being greedy and I didn't care.

"We have to go to a fundraiser tonight," I said.

"Oh." Disappointment flashed on her face. "I was hoping we could just watch television and snuggle."

"I know," I groaned. "But we still have the rest of the afternoon. C'mere." I patted the bed.

She gave me a knowing look. "I'm naked. Haven't you had enough?"

"Have you?"

"No," she admitted, blushing slightly. "I don't know what's gotten into me. I mean, I *know* what's gotten into me"—she gestured toward me—"but I don't know why I want it to get in me some more." She giggled.

I patted the bed.

She rolled her eyes. "I'm sore. Aren't you?"

"Yes. But I don't give a fuck," I said. My voice sounded strangled.

"I don't either," she said, and sighed.

AVERY

It was as though his cock was a drug. By any sane measurement, I'd had enough. But I couldn't actually *get* enough. As soon as he pulled out I felt bereft; I wanted him back inside me.

Just like I wanted him right now.

I threw the towel off and went to him stark naked. He sucked in a deep breath and shook his head. "You're so fucking beautiful, babe," he said, palming my breasts as I climbed on top of him and rubbed his erection against me. I was already wet. It was as if my body was weeping for him, wondering where he'd been.

"You're ready for me. Again." His face was smug, but as soon as I rubbed his shaft against my slit, he moaned, becoming vulnerable. I loved that about him. Big, bad quarterback Chase Layne, who could probably crush me with one hand, totally gave himself over to me when we had sex. I wrapped my fingers around the base of his erection and pumped his length. "Babe, that feels so good," he said, an unselfconscious, delighted smile on his face.

He was already thick for me. I swirled the pre-come at the tip of his luscious cock around, making sure he was lubricated. And then, not waiting, I sat up and slowly eased him inside of me. I sat down on him, taking him in inch by thick inch, until our bodies were flush.

"Oh fuck," Chase groaned, lying beneath me. "Don't even move. I'm gonna come if you do."

I started to rock against him slowly. "Go ahead—fill me up, baby. I fucking love it," I said, because I did. I'd never been with anyone as big as Chase before. He was *huge.* As soon as he was snugly inside me, my body started to vibrate. I put my palms on his massive chest and started to ride him.

This time was no exception.

He put his hands on my ass and I ground myself against him. "Babe," he said.

"Huh?" I asked, picking up speed. I cried out as he thrust into me deep.

"I'm gonna come. I'm sorry it's so soon," he said. His thumb found my clit and he rubbed it in circles.

"Oh *fuck*—don't you ever apologize," I said, and threw my head back. Waves of pleasure circled me as I continued to fuck him. I was sore and it was raw but somehow, that made it even better. My body started to move on its own accord as he went stiff and cried out a litany of curses. I moved up and down on his rigid cock, screaming as he pinched my clit, my body grinding against his shaft. I saw stars as pleasure ripped through me and everything else fell away, all my fears, my insecurities, my doubts.

"Chase!" I screamed, because I knew he liked it and I

liked it, too. His name on my lips, when I was filled with him, when I couldn't even think straight.

"Oh fuck," he grunted, his body stiff and rigid beneath mine as he emptied himself into me. He gripped my hips. "You're make me fucking crazy, babe."

Good, I thought. I leaned down and collapsed against his chest and he cradled me in his arms. He wanted *me. I* was the one who was making him crazy. He couldn't keep his hands off me.

He pulled me beside him and kissed me, his tongue seeking mine in solace. He patted my hair. "Stay with me," he said, sounding sleepy.

"For as long as you want," I promised, as I watched him fall asleep.

WE WOKE up an hour later in a panic. "Is this a black-tie fundraiser?" I asked Chase as I hustled back to the shower.

He nodded. "Do you have a dress you can wear?"

"Yeah—I just wasn't sure how fancy this was." I was nervous about going to a high-end event with a bunch of Chase's teammates, but I had to put on a brave face.

I watched him as he scrubbed his hands over his face.

"I think that Jessica and Pax are going to be there tonight. We should be prepared."

My stomach sank a little. I really just wanted to crawl back in bed with him and watch *Game of Thrones*. "You don't think he's going to try to pick another fight with you, do you?"

He shrugged. "I won't go for it if he does."

I nodded slowly. "I think our best defense might be a good offense."

Chase raised his eyebrows at me. "You're using football talk?"

I grinned at him. "I know how to get through to you."

He closed the distance between us and pulled me into his arms, making me woozy with his proximity. "You do," he admitted.

I smiled but I removed myself from his grasp. Being that close to him made a crazy heat rush through me, and I couldn't get all sweaty again. It was game time.

"I know, I know. We have to get dressed." He looked disappointed. "You were saying. A good offense?"

"That's right," I said. "We have to look great. We have to be polite. And maybe we say hello to them first. What you think about that?"

Chase grunted. "I don't want to, but someone has to be civilized. I guess it needs to happen sooner or later."

"I'll go and get dressed. You need anything?"

He shook his head, but I could see a longing in his eyes. "I'm good. I have everything that I need."

I thrilled at his words as I hustled to my room. He had managed, in a few short days, to make me feel something I'd never felt before: special.

I searched my closet, looking for a dress I remembered, a dress more beautiful than anything I'd ever seen. I dug until I found it. It was a bright blue, fitted, strapless, with a lace overlay. It looked like something a princess would wear, or an actress. I ran my fingers down the expensive fabric. This dress probably cost more than I made in a year as a waitress.

I tried it on, admiring the way it hugged my curves. Chase would love it. A little thrill ran through me at the thought of being out with him tonight, wearing something so beautiful, so proud to be at his side. I wished that every night could be like this, or rather, I wished that there were more nights like this ahead of me.

I did my makeup and fixed my hair. I put on a little extra lip gloss. *There.* I looked in the mirror approvingly. I looked as though I belonged in this dress, which, all things considered, was a minor miracle.

Chase put his hand over his heart when I came out to meet him in the foyer. "I'm pretty sure I'm having a heart attack," he said. "You're drop-dead gorgeous."

I basked in his approval. "You look nice, too. I can't

believe they make a tux that can fit all your muscles in it."

"Love the compliments—keep 'em coming." He held out his hand, and I took it gratefully. "I didn't want to go to this thing tonight, but seeing you in that dress...I take it all back."

We were quiet on the drive into the city. There was a line of limousines and hired SUVs outside of the aquarium. My stomach flipped nervously. I gripped Chase's hand. "I'm not trying to be needy, but can you help me tonight?"

"What do you mean, babe?"

"I don't want to make a fool out of myself," I said nervously. "I don't want to say anything dumb or obviously not fit in."

He squeezed my hand. "You're going to do great. Please don't be nervous. I'm going to stay beside you all night, because are you kidding me? You think I'm going to leave you alone for two seconds in that dress?" He laughed. "No way. My teammates would try to intercept you in a heartbeat."

I smiled at him warmly, his words calming me down. "Cover me."

"Now you're stealing *my* football lines?"

I giggled. "I don't actually know enough about football to know whose lines are whose."

"I'll teach you. I'll make you an expert." He squeezed my hand as the car idled at the curb. "Are you ready?"

I swallowed hard. My nerves were gathering as I watch the crowd head into the building. I nodded. "Of course," I said.

"Don't be nervous, babe. Chase has got you." His big hand squeezed mine. "Okay?"

With his hand clamped over mine like that, I felt like everything *might* actually be okay. Even though he'd referred to himself in the third person again.

"Okay."

CHAPTER 16

CHASE

I pulled Avery against me, smiling automatically for the press as the flashes went off. As soon as we got inside, I grabbed us each a glass of champagne and scanned the elegantly dressed crowd for Eric, my teammates—and Jessica and Pax. We stopped and chatted with players and other people I recognized. I proudly introduced Avery around; she was garnering lots of appreciative stares from everyone.

I didn't let go of her hand once.

Then thankfully, I saw Reggie. I'd missed my friend. "Hey buddy," I called. "I can't wait to get back to practice with you. I miss your terrorizing ways." Reggie always aggressively blocked for me at practice, often knocking several guys down in the process.

He sauntered up to me, his tuxedo looking as if it was about to burst at the seams. "You know I have to watch your back," he said, and clapped me on the shoulder.

"Not so much for my own teammates," I said, grinning at him. "Who never actually hurt me."

Reggie shook his head. "I can't help it. I see someone going for you, I automatically take them out. Can't wait until you come back tomorrow. It's been boring without you." He turned to Avery and raised his eyebrow. "But I can see you've been doing just fine."

He flashed her a smile and held out his hand. "Well, *hello*. I'm Reggie."

"I know who you are. I'm a big fan of your work." She shook his hand. "Avery Brighton."

"It's nice to meet you. You look beautiful. Even better than the pictures."

"Hey." I clamped my hand on his shoulder. "Stop trying to steal my girl."

He turned back to me, an approving look on his handsome, weathered face. "You two are looking good. I like what I see." He quickly scanned the room, and his smile turned into a grimace. "Most of it, anyway. I think I might have to take someone out *tonight*. You're going to have to hold me back." He jutted his chin in the direction of the penguins and ominously cracked his knuckles.

I turned and saw Pax and Jessica sipping champagne and regarding us coolly. I groaned. "Have you talked to him at all?"

"Hell no," Reggie said loyally. "And I don't plan to. Word is that he's getting traded. It can't happen soon enough. We're all ready to jump him and beat his ass senseless. A broken nose just isn't enough."

"He's not worth it. I should know."

Reggie shook his head. "I knew the guy had no class, but what I did *not* realize was that he's absolute trash. And Jessica...I guess she's shown her true colors. I'll leave it at that." He grunted.

I sighed as I watched Jess rub her boobs, which were spilling out of her too tight dress, against Pax's chest. "I've got nothing to say—except ugh." I reached out and grabbed Avery's hand. "Are you ready to go and face them?"

"Already?" she squeaked.

Reggie looked at me as though I'd grown an extra head. "Why're you talking to them?"

I shrugged. "I'm going to see him tomorrow at practice, anyway. A very wise person once told me that the best defense is a good offense. So we're trying that out."

Avery took a gulp of champagne. "Let's get it over with. Before I have too much to drink and start speaking my mind."

Reggie nodded and gave us a thumbs-up. "This one's a keeper. You remember I told you that."

"I'll remember. I promise."

I felt as though I was walking the plank as we headed toward Jess and Pax. Jessica inspected Avery from head to toe. Pax had dark bruises underneath his eyes, but his nose looked okay now. "Hey." I nodded at them in what I hoped was a friendly manner. "Pax, I wanted to say that I'm sorry. That was unprofessional of me to go after you like that." *Even though you fucked my wife and were taunting me about it.*

He looked taken aback. "It's...okay." He sounded unsure. Jess gave him a stern look that I was all-too-familiar with: *Stop talking.*

"This is my girlfriend, Avery Brighton. Avery, this is Jessica and Pax Unger."

"Hey," Avery said. She smiled at them.

"Chase," Jessica said, nodding at me icily. "I saw your swan boat pictures. Nice work."

"It wasn't work—I actually *like* kids. Unlike you." I took a gulp of champagne. "I saw your Instagram." I didn't say anything else.

A very awkward silence ensued.

She turned her laser-like glare to Avery. "And you... it's *interesting* to meet you. How did you two meet, again?"

"I met Chase in Harvard Square. We were book shopping."

Jess laughed. "Chase doesn't read."

Avery nodded at her, her smile still intact. "You're right—I haven't even seen him crack open the book he got that day. I think he just wanted to meet me, so he followed me into the store."

I squeezed her hand. I fucking loved this girl.

Another awkward silence ensued.

Jessica tossed her hair over her shoulder, her eyes narrowing. She turned back to me. "Mickey said you're closing on your new house soon. I need the proceeds of the sale wired into my account as soon as the Wellesley house closes. You understand that, right?"

I thought I saw Pax wince a little at either her demand or her tone, but that would mean that he had some sort of conscience. "I'll do exactly what Mickey tells me to do. Don't worry—you'll be getting all sorts of money that isn't yours real soon."

"Hey. Chase. Don't get her started," Pax said, his voice tight.

Jessica stiffened next to him. "Don't speak for me, baby. Remember what we talked about?"

Pax looked cowed and nodded obediently. "Of course."

I raised my eyebrows at him but decided not to say

anything—for his sake. "Well, we just wanted to be friendly and say hello. I go back to practice tomorrow. Avery and I are hoping that we can all be civil going forward."

Jessica was now staring Avery down. "*We?*"

I cleared my throat. "That's what I said."

Another awkward silence. "Well, see you around," I said, and hustled Avery away.

After we made it to the relative safety of the other side of the room, she chugged the rest of her champagne. "That went well."

I grimaced. "I told you she's a piece of work."

"Her boobs are, anyway. I was afraid she was going to poke my eye out with one of those things." She started to giggle, but then she seemed to get distracted by something over my shoulder.

"Holy shit." Her voice was strangled.

I turned around, searching the crowd. "What's the matter? Is Jess flying over here on her broomstick?"

"It's my sister. Oh my God, my sister's here."

She was focused on a young woman in a formfitting black dress. Her blond hair was slightly longer than Avery's and tumbled down her back in similar waves. Her eyes were blue, too.

I watched as she grabbed two flutes of champagne and took sips from them both.

"The one in the black dress? The blonde?" I asked.

Avery nodded. Her face had gone pale. "I have no idea how she got here...or where she got that dress."

"Shouldn't we go talk to her?" I asked.

Avery looked at me miserably. "Can I do it alone? I'm not ready for you to meet her."

I nodded. "I'll stay right here, but wave to me if you need backup. It's kind of weird that she's here, don't you think?"

She grimaced. "Uh...yeah." She let go of my hand and headed over, her face taut, as if she was about to face the firing squad. I watched as Lila turned and noticed her, fastening her glittering eyes on her younger sister.

I grabbed another glass of champagne even though I didn't really like the taste. I watched as Avery reached her sister and pulled her in for a hug.

Just then, Eric pulled up beside me. "Who the hell is Avery hugging?" he asked.

"Her sister." I looked at him. "By the way, hi."

"Hi yourself." He dusted the lapel of his immaculate jacket as he watched them, his brow furrowed. "Why the hell is her sister here?"

"I don't know. Avery seemed surprised." And unhappy, but I kept that to myself.

We watched as Lila proceeded to chug both the

glasses of champagne she was holding and grab two more as another server went by.

"This could be bad," Eric said, a sour look on his face.

I spotted Jessica out of the corner of my eye. She had her arms crossed against her chest, pushing her boobs up precipitously, and was appraising Avery and Lila from across the room.

I took another swig of the too sweet champagne. *Shit, shit, shit.*

"Nah," I lied.

~

AVERY

My sister looked lovely in her dress, but she was double-fisted and guzzling champagne at an alarming rate.

And she wasn't supposed to be here.

"Lila," I hiss-whispered to her. "What the hell are you doing?"

She regarded me coolly and widened her eyes in mock surprise. "Avery! I'm so happy to see you." She leaned closer and I could smell cigarette smoke in her hair. "Wouldn't it be nice if you greeted your sister in the same, friendly manner?"

"Lower your voice," I begged. "You're not supposed to

be seen in public with me. How did you even get in here?"

My sister tossed her hair over her shoulder and shrugged. "I gave the bouncer a bag of weed. I figured it was for a good cause."

"How did you find out about this?" I asked.

She snorted. "It's this little thing called the Internet—you might have heard of it."

"You have to go," I said. "If Elena finds out you were here, I'm going to get fired."

Lila took another healthy gulp of champagne. "You know that's not going to happen. The press is eating up your little story. She's not going to fire you now." She surveyed the crowd, her laser-like stare taking in every detail. "I had to come find you. You've been ignoring me. You were supposed to send me money."

"I already gave you two thousand dollars. You didn't already spend it, did you?" My panic was rising.

Lila rolled her eyes. "Not *all* of it."

"Jesus. When are you going to learn to—"

"Can you introduce me to any ballers?" she interrupted me. "I was kind of hoping I could meet one. You look like you're having so much fun, I thought I might give it a whirl."

"No, I can't. As far as they know, I don't have any family around here. Please," I said, desperate to get her to leave. "Don't ruin this for me—for us. I'm going to make so much money, I'll be able to take care of you. We'll be able to move out of that dump and get a nice apartment. But not if you mess this up."

"Where can we get an apartment?" she asked, excited. "Do you think we could move to the South End? I've always wanted to live there…"

I sighed. "Wherever you want. Just promise me you'll go."

"Not yet, okay? I got this dress from Rent the Runway for twenty-five bucks," she said as she smoothed it. "It needs to earn out. Plus, there's free drinks."

She chugged some more champagne. "Bottoms up," she said. "Oops, looks like we've got company. He's *huge* in real life, huh?" Looking past me and gawking.

Chase was suddenly beside me. I felt relieved that he was close, but I kept my face neutral. I didn't want my sister to see my feelings written all over my face. Any sort of ammunition she could assemble would be dangerous, potentially lethal. "You must be Avery's sister," he said in a friendly tone, holding his hand out for Lila. "I'm Chase Layne. I've heard so much about you."

"Don't believe a word of it." Lila shook his hand and simultaneously stuck her chest out at him. I winced and

Chase protectively snaked his arm around my waist, a fact that was not lost on Lila's wandering eyes. "It's so nice to finally meet *you*, Chase. Avery's been hiding you from me—or me from you. I'm not sure which."

"Lila was just finishing her drink and leaving," I said pointedly.

My sister shook her head. "I'm not ready to go. I haven't met anybody, and I haven't had all the free champagne I can handle yet," she whined.

"My driver's available now, if you'd like him to take you home. It's a sweet ride—an Escalade, brand new." Chase smiled at her. He'd just met her, but he already had my sister's number.

That seemed to perk Lila up. She turned her gaze to me. "Ave, do you have any cash I can borrow? Maybe I can have the driver drop me at this club I've been wanting to check out. Since I'm all dressed."

I nodded stiffly, feeling my face turn a molten red. "Sure. I'll walk you out and make sure you have everything you need." I turned to Chase, certain he could read the humiliation on my face. "Be right back."

"I'll wait for you in the lobby." He kissed me briefly on the forehead and surreptitiously stuffed a handful of bills into my hand.

I turned back to find my sister watching us, clearly fascinated. "Let's go," I said in defeat. I hustled her toward the lobby. It didn't matter where I was in life, my sister would always be waiting to drag me back down.

"He seems fond of you," she said. "He must really enjoy having live-in...*help.*"

I winced. "Why would you say something mean like that?"

"Because I'm your sister, and somebody needs to look out for you. I saw the puppy-dog look you just gave him," she said. "You seem like you're doing more than just your job. Someone needs to remind you of who you *really* are, and where you're going back to when Prince Charming cuts you loose."

This was classic Lila. She was acting as though she were looking out for me, but really, she was just putting me down. "I don't know why you have to treat me that way. All I've ever tried to do is take care of you."

"Don't be so sensitive," Lila said. "I'm trying to help you." She tossed her hair, giving the party a last, longing once-over. "Wait a minute—is that Pax Unger? And Jessica Layne?"

I turned to find them watching us. I nodded, feeling sick. "Yes."

"Interesting," my sister said. I put the stack of bills into her hand. "Please use some of this for groceries, and not just weed, cigarettes, and Jim Beam."

Lila gave me a tight smile. "I'll see what I can do."

With that, she sashayed out the door, coolly nodding at Jessica and Pax before she left.

Chase came up next to me and my stomach sank. "I think she's planning something," I said. "You're going to wish you never met me."

He put his arm around me and pulled me against him. "It's okay, babe. We'll go home and you can tell me about her."

"Great," I said, feeling the happy buzz from the last few days wear off. *Just fucking great.*

CHAPTER 17

CHASE

"So…she does drugs?"

Avery nodded miserably.

"Like what?"

She shrugged. "She smokes pot. And drinks a lot. I think that's it. But she's never been able to hold down a job. She's not responsible enough." I watched her throat work as she swallowed.

"And you take care of her?"

"She took it hard when our mom died. It's like she's still angry about it…" Avery's voice trailed off. "I was hoping I could get her into some sort of rehab program with the money from this assignment. She's not a bad person. I think she just needs help."

I nodded, but I had a pit in my stomach. If I hadn't

liked the way Lila was looking at Avery, I sure as shit didn't like the way Jess was looking at Lila. "What did she say to you? Why was she there tonight?"

Avery appeared as though she was going to cry. "She wants money. She wants me to give her money so she can go shopping and do…whatever it is she does."

"I only gave her about a thousand," I said, referring to the bills I'd handed to Avery earlier. "Is that enough?"

"I already gave her two thousand earlier this week," Avery said, her voice flat, "so I'm thinking no."

"She's knows you're on an assignment, right?" My voice was tight.

She picked at some invisible lint on the T-shirt she'd changed into. "Yep."

I cracked open a beer. "This isn't good. If she went public—"

"She won't," Avery said, interrupting me. "I'll give her whatever she wants. I won't let her do that to you."

I took a sip of beer. "I'm sorry she's like that. And that you have to deal with her."

Avery raised her eyes to mine. "Not as sorry as I am."

"Maybe I can help…" I let my voice trail off. I didn't know what to say. I really didn't want to get involved with the sister. I could tell she was bad news. She was also probably a black hole—if I started giving her money, she'd never go away.

She shook her head. "That's not your responsibility. I'll deal with it."

After I finished my beer, we listlessly went to bed. "I can't watch the show," I mumbled. "Practice early." I crawled under the covers and motioned for her to join me. Our earlier high had come crashing down, and now I just felt exhausted.

"S'okay," Avery said, coming close to me but not touching. "I'm tired, anyway."

"Good night," I said. It sounded awkward and formal.

"Good night."

~

AVERY

Of course, I couldn't sleep. Images of my sister in her rented dress kept swirling in my mind, as well as images of Jess and Pax inspecting her.

She was a liability and I knew it.

What was worse, *Chase* knew it. And it seemed to bother him.

I rolled over and watched him sleep. Lila wasn't a bad person; she just wasn't always a good person. But I'd meant what I said—I wouldn't let her hurt him. His powerful chest rose and fell rhythmically and I studied him, mesmerized. I wouldn't let anyone hurt him.

Especially not me.

AFTER A FITFUL NIGHT'S SLEEP, I woke up to find Chase already out of bed. I stumbled out and found him in the kitchen.

"Hey," he said. "Want some coffee?"

I nodded, trying to gauge his mood. "Are you happy about going back to practice?"

"Oh yeah." He looked so excited that I relaxed, even though I hadn't been fully aware that I was tense. "Can't wait. Would you like to come with me?"

I perked up. "Can I?"

"Sure—it's fun. A lot of fans come out to watch us practice. It's free, and it's a great way to get them excited about the season." He checked his phone. "Eric said he expects a record turnout today because I'm going back, and Pax is going to be there."

"Oh boy."

"It'll be all right," Chase said, easily. He seemed back to his normal, upbeat self. "Coach will keep us separated. I just have to keep Reggie occupied so he doesn't pummel him."

"Reggie will just be psyched that you're back," I said.

"That's true." He smiled at me, and it was like the sun coming out.

I quickly put on a pair of jean shorts and a Warriors T-shirt, my hair pulled up into a bun. We took Chase's truck to the stadium. He was quiet on the way in.

"Are you nervous?" I asked.

"Not at all." He shook his head. "I can't wait. I've missed it."

Warriors Arena was enormous, surrounded by parks and a plaza with restaurants, shops, and bars. Chase hustled me to the entrance of the practice fields, taking in the group of players already waiting for him. He turned to me, grinning. He was clearly in his element.

"Okay. You go up and sit in the stands and cheer for me. Real loud, like I like it." He leaned down as if he was about to kiss me. "Thank you for being here," he said, with a look that melted me. "It means a lot."

I smiled at him, feeling as though things were back to normal between us. "Are you kidding me? This is awesome!"

"Then you should come with me every day. I seriously love having you here, babe."

He put his hands in my hair, leaning over me, and then crushed his lips against mine. It felt so hot between us I was worried my shorts were on fire. "Mmm," Chase murmured, pulling away too soon. "We need to do more of that later. We wasted too much time sleeping last night."

I stared up at him, feeling woozy. I forced myself to snap out of it. "Chase Layne, you stop that right now. Get over there and see your teammates."

He laughed. "Chase Layne hates to leave you. But he has to go." With a parting nod, he ran off happily toward his team, as if he was a little boy and couldn't wait to practice.

I climbed into the rapidly filling stands and sat with the rest of the fans. A lot of them gave me curious stares. One woman in particular kept looking at at me, trying to make eye contact.

I finally turned to her. "Hi," I said awkwardly.

"Hi!" She was obviously thrilled that I acknowledged her. "You're Chase's girlfriend, right?"

"Right." I felt stupidly proud.

"We"—she said, motioning to the rows of fans all around us—"are *so* excited that Chase seems happy. It's a terrible shame about that wife of his. Ex-wife, I mean." She looked momentarily chastised, but I just shrugged, trying to indicate it was fine. She leaned forward conspiratorially. "I never saw her smiling, that one. It was like she was too good for him." She snorted. "As *if*." Seemingly satisfied, she turned back toward the practice.

I watched too, mesmerized. Chase was out there, glorious and muscled, in the center of the field. I couldn't help staring at his calves. They were huge. I guess I hadn't noticed them before, but with his football pants on, they were accentuated, glistening in the sun and straining beneath the fabric.

I mentally slapped myself. Here I was, sitting at training camp for the Warriors, drooling over the quarterback. I forced myself to stop ogling his calves and take in my surroundings. The stands had filled already, and the grass nearby was quickly being covered by picnic blankets and eager fans. There were hotdog vendors and places to buy slushies; the air of excitement was palpable in the crowd.

I watched as Chase deftly threw a pass, the ball sailing down the field to Reggie, who caught it easily. Smiling, Chase turned to look for me in the stands and our eyes briefly connected. My heart leapt.

I hated to admit it to myself, because I knew it was going to hurt later—but even with the Lila drama, and the fact that I was Chase's fake girlfriend, this was hands-down the best week of my life.

That was sad. It was also true.

Practice continued through the morning and eventually they took a break. Some of the fans had autographs signed by Chase and the other players. And then I saw a very attractive, albeit overdressed, woman with long dark hair make her way out to the field and drape her arms around one of the players.

Oh shit. It was Jessica Layne.

One of Chase's teammates came up and whispered in his ear as he chatted with the fans. Chase shot a wary glance over his shoulder. I took a deep breath and headed down to see him. I could see Jessica and Pax still out on the field, their arms around each other, having a full-blown make-out session, violating every ethical and moral code that a wife and a teammate should hold dear.

Chase leaned over me when I finally got to him. "I can't believe they're doing this," he said. "It's so unprofessional."

"I know," I said. I looked over his massive shoulder and caught Jessica staring our way, her gaze flicking curiously over me. I turned back to Chase and grabbed his hand. I didn't want his first practice back ruined. "You're playing really well," I offered. "Everybody in the stands is raving about you. And one woman even told me she was happy you're getting a divorce. The fans are *not* loving Jess right now."

"Well, that's good I guess." He shot another look over his shoulder, where they were still engaged in a very public display of affection. "I just want him off my team."

I squeezed his hand again. "I know." I went back to my seats, my stomach roiling on Chase's behalf. I watched as Jessica strutted back across the field in her inappropriately sexy dress and took her place in the stands.

The woman who'd spoken to me earlier leaned over. "Did you see that?" she hissed. "Absolutely no respect for this team. They ought to throw her out."

I grimaced in agreement.

As I watched the practice continue, something was clear to me—Jessica wanted to hurt Chase. Bad.

I had to make sure she didn't get to my sister.

That would be a disaster.

CHAPTER 18

CHASE

I made some phone calls that afternoon and just sort of wandered around in a foul mood. Jessica and Pax had gotten to me today. And the sister had gotten to me last night.

Just when I'd thought everything was looking up...

Eric called me. "Hey buddy."

"Hey." I cracked open a beer and stalked out to my patio.

"I talked to Wes—they're trading Pax this week. They made the call right after that stunt he and Jess pulled at practice. Tim fully endorsed it."

I sat down heavily. "Good."

"You okay?" Eric asked.

I took a swig of beer. "I just want this to be over with.

174

Jess's seriously trying to fuck with me. I don't even get the point. She's getting a ton of my money. Why would she pull that shit at practice? I can't wrap my head around what she's doing."

"I have an idea...but you're not going to like it."

"Just tell me." I had more beer to ward off a threatening headache.

"I heard through the grapevine that she and Pax are shopping a reality show around," Eric said. "I think she's trying to get as much attention as possible to drum up interest from the networks."

"Great," I groaned. "So I can be featured as an off-screen villain while she and Pax prance half-naked around a pool."

"Maybe." Eric sighed. "Probably."

"What sucks is that they just won't go away. They'll ride this pathetic wave as far as they can."

"I know," Eric said. "It does suck."

"It's good that you hired Avery for me," I offered, trying to find a bright side. "At least I'm faring well in the hot new girlfriend department. The team seems good, too. They were totally supportive today. It was awesome to be back."

"Good," Eric said, his voice neutral. "But I think they would have been anyway. I don't think Avery changed that. I think she just changed how you *feel* about it. I don't know how much actual credit she gets."

I bristled at his words. "I thought that was the plan—I was supposed to appear like I was in control, and the rest would fall into place. Remember? Your little pep talk? When you talked me into this in the first place?" My voice was rising. He was seriously on the verge of poking the Chase Layne bear. "What are you saying now—that this was a bad idea?"

"No—hey, calm down," Eric said. "I'm just concerned."

"About what?" I barked.

"That she's becoming a liability," he said quietly. "The sister has me worried. The fact that she showed up at that function bothers me."

My stomach sank. Eric was saying what I'd been thinking for the past twenty-four hours. "She asked Avery for money," I said.

"Fuck," Eric said. "What's her deal?"

I drained my beer. "She doesn't work. She sponges off Avery. She's greedy and cares more about weed and nice clothes than she does that her baby sister's out turning tricks to pay their rent."

"That's just fucking great," Eric said. "Does the sister know? About you?"

"Yeah."

My agent went quiet for a minute, digesting the news. "So what's the play?" he finally asked.

"Avery said she was taking care of it."

"That might not be good enough," Eric said.

I thought of Jess, watching Avery and Lila, her arms crossed against her chest.

"I know," I said.

AVERY

I was headed to the kitchen when I heard Chase yelling out back. I went toward the door and then froze. "Remember? Your little pep talk?" he barked into his phone. "When you talked me into this in the first place?"

I opened my mouth and then closed it, listening to the rest of the conversation even though I knew it was wrong.

She asked Avery for money.

She doesn't work...sponges off Avery...doesn't care that her baby sister's turning tricks...

And the clincher. *This was a bad idea.*

He was talking about me. And Lila. And he didn't sound happy about any of it. In fact, he sounded positively furious.

I looked out the window and saw his face, which was

normally open and happy. It was now pinched and angry.

I fled for the relative sanctuary of my room. A jumble of emotions fought for dominant position inside me as I paced, wringing my hands together.

Lila was ruining everything. But what else was new?

What was I really upset about?

I needed the money from this assignment. If I didn't get it, I would have to keep hooking. There was no other way I was going to make ends meet. I didn't have anyone to take me in, Lila didn't seem interested in earning a paycheck, and my landlord certainly wouldn't do us any favors.

But even though the money was the reason I was here, it wasn't the thing I cared about. That's not why I was in my room, pacing, on the verge of tears.

It was Chase. It was his tone, discussing me as if I were a stranger. An inconvenient problem to be solved.

The hired help.

I thought I'd felt something real between us over the last few days. It was the way he'd looked at me, held me, called me *babe*. Was that all an act? So he could get laid?

A star NFL quarterback, a gorgeous one, didn't need to manipulate their way into lady parts. Or pay to get in there, for that matter. But was that what Chase was doing? Even though he'd bought my services, did he feel like it was necessary to *charm* me first? To assuage his guilt?

Mr. Golden Boy couldn't deal with fucking a hooker, so he made it seem like he was winning me over... Was that true? Is that what had happened between us?

I stopped pacing and looked at myself in the mirror. That wasn't what had happened to *me*. It was something much worse.

It was real feelings.

I WENT to practice with Chase every day. I hadn't told him about the conversation I'd overheard because I didn't know what to say. Pax was gone, traded to Tennessee. Jess had gone with him and was posting their every carefully choreographed and filtered move to social media.

We settled into a routine, but I felt *unsettled*. Chase was right next to me, but I didn't know what he was thinking. I also didn't know how long our arrangement would continue to last, or how I was going to deal with it ending.

Real feelings were a real pain in the ass.

I made dinner every night. Chase and I were back to binge-watching *Game of Thrones*. The characters were being treated egregiously, in my opinion. I'd started watching with the covers pulled up to my nose. Bad things kept happening. But still, I couldn't turn away.

I was in too deep now. I cared too much.

We were back to having sex, too. But it was different. Now every time I came, I felt like I was going to cry. Emotions were a seriously messed up thing. As far as I was concerned, mine could go fly a kite.

Chase closed on the new house. He seemed excited. I felt…like I was going to cry.

The landline rang while Chase was in the shower. I would've never thought of answering it, but I was standing right there and checked the Caller ID in case it was Eric. It wasn't—but it *was* a number I immediately recognized. My heart stopped.

"Lila?" I answered the phone. "How did you get this number?"

"I have my ways," she said. "Besides, you told me never to use your cell phone again."

I took a deep breath, willing myself to calm down and simultaneously preparing for the worst. "What's up?"

"You haven't been in touch," she said, her tone wheedling. "I feel like you're cutting me out. You finally got a piece of something nice, and now you don't want anything to do with me."

Actress, my head warned, but I still felt my heart wrench. "I'm sorry. I haven't done anything to try to hurt you on purpose. If it seems like I'm distancing myself, I'm only doing it to protect this job."

"You don't have to lie to me, you know. I think you care a lot about Chase. Admit it."

I would admit nothing of the kind to my sister. "I'm just trying to help him by making this look real. And to make enough money that I never have to hook again."

"When're you coming home?" she asked.

"I don't know." I didn't want to think about it.

"Well, I need more money between now and whenever that is."

"How much more?"

"Two million." Lila sounded casually defiant.

"Two million *dollars*?" She was insane. "You're kidding, right?"

"I am not kidding. Tell your pretend boyfriend I want two million dollars, or I'm going public with your story."

"Lila...you can't do this to me," I said, my voice strangled.

"I'm doing it for us," she said. "To protect our future."

I was shaking. My sister. My greedy fucking sister. "You can't go public and you know it. I told you I signed a confidentiality agreement. If we breach that, we won't get anything. I won't ever even get paid. And they'll come after us. Who wins then?"

"I want you to consider what I'm telling you. Because I'm *not* kidding," Lila said, her voice even. "Chase Layne has plenty of money. He doesn't need it. From what I've read, he gives to charities left and right. Let him give some of that money to *us*. And don't worry about your confidentiality agreement—this is blackmail. It isn't covered in some contract clause."

I felt like the floor was going to drop out from beneath me.

"I am *not* going to ask him for that amount of money. Over my dead body." My voice was shaking.

"You should think about what I'm saying," Lila said, her voice soothing. "It makes sense. We need to think about ourselves. An opportunity like this isn't ever going to knock again."

"You are not a charity case. It's time you grew up and stopped taking advantage of other people. Otherwise, you'll be a dirty old grifter before you know it. Just like mom." I struggled to catch my breath.

"Shut your mouth," she hissed, all pretense of soothing gone. "You do not dare talk to me like that."

"I'm probably long past due talking to you like this."

"It figures you'd bring up mom. You never had any sympathy for her. She was a *junkie*. She was *sick*. And you walked around like you were ashamed of her. You never loved her like I did."

"Shut *up*," I said, but deep in my heart, I worried that what she'd said was true. My mother had humiliated me. I thought of her addiction as a weakness, a fault.

But that guilt was my cross to bear. I couldn't let me sister use it against me right now.

"I'm the one who was cleaning up her mess the whole time she was using. And now I'm doing it all over again with you. But I'm *done*. All this time, I thought I was protecting you. That sooner or later, you were going to grow up and be the kind of sister I'd always wanted. Someone I could trust."

A chill went through me and I shivered. "And look at what I get."

Chase walked in then, a questioning look on his face.

"I have to go. I'll call you later."

"Don't forget about me," she said.

Like I could be that lucky.

CHAPTER 19

CHASE

"Everything okay?" I asked. I could tell from Avery's pale face that everything was far from it, but I waited for her answer.

"No. But it will be."

"Can I help?"

Avery shook her head. "I don't think so."

"Do you want to have a drink?" She looked as though she could use one.

She nodded, her chin wobbling a little.

I poured her a glass of wine and motioned for her to sit on my lap. "C'mere. Come to Chase."

She warily obeyed and I wrapped my arms around her. I kissed the top of her head. "Was that your sister?"

She shrugged and nestled against my chest. "I don't want to talk about it."

"Why not?"

She started playing with my hair. "Because I don't want to talk. I just want to be with you."

My cock immediately sprang to life, even as an alarm was going off in my head.

"Take me to bed," Avery whispered in my ear.

I immediately picked her up and carried her to my room. And then I made love to her, slowly, deeply, my body saying all the things I didn't dare to.

ERIC MADE me go for a run with him. "You run too slow," I complained, as we headed down the path next to the Charles River.

He tried to smile at me as he panted. "That'll give us more time to talk."

"Great. Talk about what?"

"My favorite client." Eric checked his iWatch. The pussy was probably monitoring his heart rate. "I have more news about Jess and Pax. They're closing in on a network deal."

"That's just great," I grunted.

"It has me thinking…" he said. "I'm worried about

Avery. I'm worried they're going to find out about her and use the information against you."

I glared at him. "You're worrying about that *now*? Shouldn't you have thought of it earlier?"

"*Earlier* I wasn't worried about you getting serious about her." He huffed next to me.

"I'm not getting serious about her." I looked straight ahead.

"So…if I tell you that I don't think you need her anymore, will you be willing to cut her loose?" Eric asked.

"Right now?" I asked. Panic filled my chest.

"Yep. Right now."

"I think that's premature," I said, still not looking at him.

"Uh-huh. I thought so, buddy."

"Shut up, Eric."

"I can't breathe, anyway. I'm gonna have to."

"That's the best news I've heard all day," I said.

ONE OF THE perks of being an NFL quarterback with lots of endorsement deals was that you could afford movers. And decorators. And you could pay them to do things extra-fast.

We were in my new house almost as soon as the ink was dry on the contract.

I was examining my wine refrigerator when there was a knock on the door. I looked at my watch; it was six p.m. I cautiously approached the security camera and peered at it. We weren't expecting anyone.

There, on the front step, the person I feared the most.

My mother. Looking indignant.

"Oh God," I groaned.

Avery looked at me worriedly. "Who is it?" She got pale. "Is it my sister?"

"No. It's worse." My shoulders slumped. "It's my mother. And she's upset with me because I haven't introduced you to her yet. Or invited her to see the new house."

Avery raised her eyebrows. "Oh boy." She was quiet for a second, biting her lip. "She doesn't...*know* about me, does she?"

"Hell no," I said. "Not that my mother would judge you—she's not like that."

I looked at the door, panic-stricken. I wasn't going to tell her anything, but I couldn't underestimate my mother's ability to find shit out. "I have to let her in now. It'll be fine. Trust me."

Avery nodded nervously as I swung the door open.

"Ma!" I said, taking my mom in my arms and giving her a hug. "You should've called! I would've sent a car."

"I figured I had to surprise you, or you'd say you were too busy for me." Martha pulled back from me and adjusted her lavender-rimmed, owl-like glasses. Her blond hair was pulled back in a demure headband, and she was wearing a yellow button-down sweater. If you didn't know her, she would look like your average, Volvo-driving, preppy, middle-aged woman. The truth was, she was a ruthlessly plainspoken, proud, tiger cat of a mom. I started to internally sweat. I hope she liked Avery. She'd *hated* Jessica, and it had been a disaster from the beginning.

I didn't have time to wonder why I was so concerned about my mother approving of my fake girlfriend.

"I'm assuming this is your girlfriend?" she asked, gesturing to Avery. She looked her up and down. "The one you've been keeping from me?"

Avery smiled at her cautiously. She shook my mother's hand. "It's a pleasure to meet you, Mrs. Layne."

Martha smiled back at her. "*Finally*," she said, making her way into the house.

"This is lovely." She clucked her tongue as she looked around the entryway and headed into the kitchen. "Very nice. Too bad I had to come down and ambush you in order to see it. I've been feeling more than a little left out lately, honey."

"Aw, I'm sorry," I said. "There's just been so much going on."

"It's been sort of a whirlwind," Avery agreed.

Martha turned to Avery, inspecting her carefully, as if she were an expensive organic melon at a farmer's market. "Is this something you're used to? This lifestyle? The limelight?"

She shook her head. "No, ma'am."

My mother crossed her arms against her chest and eyed her with suspicion. "You seem like you're adjusting pretty well."

"Uh...let me show you the living room," I said, hustling my mother toward it.

"I'm going to let you two catch up." Avery retreated toward the kitchen. "Mrs. Layne, are you hungry? I was just about to make dinner."

"I could eat," Martha said. She didn't sound as grateful as I wished she had, but it was at least a start.

"You don't have to grill her, Ma. Avery's on my team." I sat down heavily on the couch and patted the chair next to me. My mother sat down warily, watching my face.

"You two seem pretty serious. At least from all the pictures I've seen," she sniffed.

I shrugged. "She's really sweet. She makes me happy." When I said it out loud to my mom, I realized how true it was.

"That's good, " Martha said. "I just want you to be careful this time. I don't want to see you go through what you went through with Jessica again."

"I won't." I leaned forward. "Avery isn't anything like that."

Martha was quiet for a moment, picking invisible lint off her clothes. "I spoke to Eric."

My heart squeezed. Eric couldn't have told her the truth about Avery. He wouldn't.

"He's worried about you." Her voice was neutral.

"Oh yeah? Why is that?" My throat felt tight.

My mom looked up at me, a sad look on her face. "Are you really planning on lying to me, Chase? Your own mother?"

"Lying to you about what?"

"Lying about Avery," she said. She looked crestfallen. "Eric told me the truth. That he'd hired this girl for you."

I swallowed hard. I opened my mouth and then closed it. *Fucking Eric.*

Martha shook her head. "A *prostitute*? How could you disrespect women like that?"

"It's not like that," I said. "Eric hired her to pretend she was my girlfriend. We thought it would be a good counterattack to what Jessica and Pax were doing. It was never a sexual arrangement, mom. I was never paying her for sex." I winced and felt myself redden. I was pretty sure my mother and I hadn't had a conversation which included the word 'sex' since our mutually humiliating birds-and-bees talk in sixth grade.

"But you're still paying her, right?" Martha asked gently. "And you're having sex with her now?"

"*Mom.*" I clenched my hands into fists. "Enough. And just wait until I get my hands on Eric—"

"The reason Eric told me is because he's your friend. And he's worried about you," she interrupted me. "He's worried that you care about her. And that the press is going to find out who she really is and that your career is never going to recover."

I swallowed hard. "Eric should've thought of that before he hired her." *I should have, too.*

"I don't think he was thinking or planning on you falling in love with her."

"Who said I was in love with her?"

My mother patted my hand. "You are gorgeous, brilliant and talented," she said, "but sometimes you need a little help."

AVERY

I watched warily as Martha entered the kitchen. "So Eric told you?" I wiped down a countertop that was already clean. "I overheard. I figure I wouldn't be so good at pretending I hadn't."

She nodded at me sympathetically. "I am not one to judge, hon. I've only met you tonight, but I can already tell you're much nicer than that Jessica. She was a real piece of work." She sat down on one of the barstools and watched as I prepared a skirt steak for Chase. "Can I help? I can make a salad just the way he likes."

I nodded at her, feeling guarded. "Sure." What I wanted to say was that I would love to know how to make Chase's favorite salad because I wanted—more than anything—to be able to do those sorts of things for him, even though I was a prostitute from the wrong side of the tracks. Even though there was an expiration date on our relationship. On our fake relationship.

Martha got up and assembled a line of vegetables, and then settled herself back down at the island with a cutting board. She chopped calmly, and the silence was not uncomfortable. "So," she said, "do you love my son?"

"Huh?"

She looked up and pursed her lips. "You might as well answer."

I leaned back against the countertop and blew out a

defeated breath. Now I understood why Chase had looked panicked when she'd shown up on his doorstep.

"I genuinely respect and care for your son, Mrs. Layne."

She went back to the vegetables. "But?"

"*But* I don't think that I'm the right person for him, even though I wish I was." Saying it out loud made my heart hurt.

"I'm happy to see that you're feeding him. At least you got that part right." Martha concentrated on chopping a cucumber—then the carrots, then the mushrooms, then the beets. I had no idea what she was thinking. I also had no idea that Chase enjoyed beets, which I found foreign and vaguely disgusting. After a few minutes, she raised her eyes to meet mine as she put the vegetables neatly into the salad bowl. "I've never seen my son like this with a woman before," she said.

I started. "What about Jessica? He said that he was so into her in the beginning that he didn't see all the screaming, neon signs that she was trouble."

"Jessica was a pain from the beginning. Chase didn't see it, that's true. But that's because I think she did some things for him in bed that nobody else had done before." I felt myself start to blush, and Martha shook her head at me. "I don't like to stick my nose too far into my son's personal life. I'm just telling you what I saw. And what I see now."

I crossed my arms against my chest. "So what do you see now?" That stupid, hopeful bird was fluttering around my chest again, suddenly frenzied.

I was going to have to take it out back and shoot it sooner rather than later.

"He proposed to Jessica because she gave him an ultimatum. He also thought she made him look good. I think with *that* relationship, my son made the mistake of being more rational than emotional. The opposite is true with you. I can tell he cares about you even though he knows it's not the right thing for his career. That's not like my son. Nothing is more important to Chase than football."

I nodded at her, feeling miserable.

She regarded me for a moment. "Do you love my son? I'm not going to ask you again."

I tried to keep my face mask-like. But what the hell? Was the truth going to hurt any more than another lie?

"Of course I love him," I said finally. "But I don't *want* to love him."

Martha nodded and adjusted her lavender-framed glasses. "It's nice to see that my son actually does have good taste. After that Jessica, I had some real questions."

She turned toward the living room. "Chase!" She hollered. "Dinner!"

CHASE

When she left later that night, my mother only had one thing to say about Avery. "She's good people." She patted me on the arm. "I approve, dear. You should always run them by me first. I'm your mother, and I really do know best."

"So you...*like* her?"

Martha nodded. "You can't always choose who you love. And I don't think it's wise to judge someone's circumstances so harshly. That doesn't mean this is going to be easy. But I'm also assuming a lot right now by even saying that."

"What do you mean?"

"I *mean* it's assuming a lot to say that she'll have a relationship with you." Martha shook her head. "She seems certain that she's bad for you and your career. From what I saw, that's going to be a big problem. Because she puts you first."

"Huh. Wow." I looked at my mother, flabbergasted. "How'd you get to be so smart, mom?"

"Because I always had to stay two steps ahead of you

for your own good." She hugged me then headed out the door. "You're going to have to convince her that she's more important to you than your career. And I honestly don't know if you're capable of that. I will tell you, however, that I'm a big fan of a happy ending. See what you can do for your poor neglected mother."

I kissed her good-bye and then closed the door, resting against it heavily, thinking about what my mom had said.

I truly sucked at lying. In order for me to convince Avery that she was more important to me than football, that would have to be true. *Was it?* If the truth came out about her background and that I'd hired her, my position as the NFL's reigning golden boy would be seriously compromised. It would also create a press feeding frenzy that could critically impact both my team and my season—exactly what I'd hired her to avoid in the first place.

Could I give up my whole future, my pristine reputation, everything that I've been working toward my whole life?

As usual, my mother was right. My heart told me that the jury was still out on that particular question. I wanted them both. I wanted it all.

CHAPTER 20

AVERY

Lila: We need 2 talk

Avery: I'll call you soon

I sighed and threw the phone onto the couch. I'd been dealing with my sister for the past few days by not dealing with her, even though I knew that was a mistake. I'd told her I was busy with the move. We hadn't spoken, just texted. She hadn't mentioned anything else about her outrageous request, but I knew she was only biding her time.

I didn't want to think about Lila anymore; I would call her in a little while. I decided to fire up Chase's laptop and do a quick Internet search for any news on Jessica and Pax, who had been unusually quiet for the past couple of days. I scrolled through some press releases about him joining Tennessee, a statement from his agent about the trade, and some other football stuff. Then I went to an image search and looked at dozens of pictures of him and Jessica. She really was a piece of work. Her pictures demonstrated that clearly. In each shot, her hand was expertly at her hip, and her chest was thrust out forcefully. She was beautiful at first glance, but there was nothing warm or friendly about her.

I went to Jessica's Instagram feed in spite of my better judgment. There was a bunch of pictures posted of their new home in Tennessee and of Jessica in a bikini out by the new pool. But one picture made me stop— and I wondered if I was hallucinating. It was another one of Jessica in a bikini and Pax grilling in the background. At first glance, nothing was unusual or alarming about it.

But what was behind Pax made my heart stop. It was a woman's profile.

My sister's profile.

I picked up my cell phone again and desperately tried to call her. It went straight to voicemail. Then I sent her another text.

Avery: Call me as soon as you can. 911.

And then I got up and started pacing.

I knew that was Lila in the picture. She must be in Tennessee with Jessica and Pax. Maybe they'd offered her the money she was looking for. My brain felt like it was being scrambled. How had she gotten in touch with them? Was she staying with them?

And oh my God, what on Earth had she told them?

I felt the blood drain from my face and I sat down heavily. I still hadn't told Chase that Lila had threatened blackmail. There were several reasons for that. I was hoping I could talk her out of it and that she would come to her senses. I was worried that he would just offer to pay her and then she'd never stop using him.

Mostly, I was afraid that it would make him hate me and want to distance himself from me and my toxic family.

Now my sister had done an end-run around me to Chase's soon-to-be-ex-wife. She was going to ruin everything. *No wait,* I thought, *you're the one wrecking everything. You're the hooker.*

You're the problem, and you're the one that's going to ruin Chase's life.

I had to get out of his house and away from Chase. I couldn't do this to him. I believed that deep down, he cared about me, but no one wanted this sort of destruction. He put his career first, and I just wasn't worth the risk. I came from nothing and had nothing to offer him, except for his downfall.

I ran up the stairs and started packing.

CHASE

I came back from a team meeting, starving. I wondered if Avery wanted to go to the North End for *pasta all'Arrabiatta* and steamed mussels. And fresh bread. And cannolis from Mike's Pastry...

"Babe?" I called. She didn't answer. I poked my head into the kitchen, and not finding her there, I bounded up the stairs. "Ave? Are you up here?" I opened the bedroom door and saw her raggedly zipping up a suitcase.

My heart stopped. "What're you doing?"

She wouldn't look at me. She kept wrestling with the zipper, finally getting around the corner and securing the suitcase. "I have to go."

"Go where?"

She looked at me wiped the sweat from her forehead. Then she put her hands on her hips. "To my boyfriend's."

I felt as if I'd been punched in the gut, hard. "What?"

Her eyes were cold, distant. "I *said,* I'm going to my boyfriend's house. My real boyfriend's house."

I opened my mouth and closed it. Then I took a step back and leaned against the wall for support. "What the fuck are you saying to me?"

"I have some other bad news for you," she said, and now her voice was shaking. "I saw a picture of Jessica and Pax today. I think my sister's at their house."

I opened my mouth again to speak but nothing came out.

She took a step toward me, her eyes softening a fraction. "I am *so* sorry for the trouble I've caused you. I don't know what she's doing, but obviously, it's going to be terrible. I didn't tell you...she asked me for money. Lots of money. Or she said she'd tell the press about me."

"How much?"

"Two million dollars."

"When the hell did she do *that*?"

Her eyes searched mine. "A few days ago."

"Babe." I slumped back against the wall. "Why didn't you tell me? At least give me the opportunity to do some damage control?"

"I didn't want you to know." Now her eyes filled with tears. "I didn't want you to hate me."

"I could never hate you—"

"But I heard you. On the phone with Eric. Talking about me and Lila."

I shook my head. "So? I told him that I didn't trust her, and that I thought she was taking advantage of you—"

"I heard you say it was a *bad idea*," she cut me off. "That hiring me was a bad idea."

"That was Eric. And that's not what he said. Not exactly." My heart was pounding in my chest. *He said he was worried you were becoming a liability. Which was exactly what I'd been thinking.* I could feel myself turning red with shame.

"It doesn't really matter. You know it's true." Her voice shook.

"No it's not—"

"You don't even know all the bad things about me. About my family," she said, cutting me off again. "And you don't want to know." Now she was crying.

"Of course I want to know—" I reached for her.

She took a step back and wiped her face roughly. "Really? You want to know that my mother was a *junkie*? That she overdosed my senior year of high school? That she used to bring home dirty men to have sex with so they'd pay for her drugs? Doesn't that make me just *perfect* for you, Mr. Golden Boy?"

I felt as though my heart was going to break. "Babe.

I'm so sorry. I didn't know. Please."

"Of course you didn't know! Why would anyone want to know something that ugly?"

"I want to know. I care—"

"Even your own mother said that you aren't thinking straight right now. That nothing's more important to you than football."

I raised my hands in exasperation. "My mother *loves* you. And you already know there's nothing more important to me than football."

She took another step back and nodded. "You're right. I do." It was as though an iceberg had erupted between us, shooting up from the floor.

Chase Layne was royally fucking this up.

She grabbed her suitcase and headed toward the door. "I'm sorry about my sister. She wants to talk to me. I'll see what I can do to make her come to her senses." I could see the muscles in her throat work as she swallowed. "I know you'll never be able to forgive me for this, but that's nothing in comparison to how I feel about myself. So I'm going now."

Oh, fuck no. This was spiraling out of control.

I stepped in front of her. I felt terrible about Avery's mother, but I also felt desperate. And angry. "So you're running off to your boyfriend's house—your *real* boyfriend's house—to lick your wounds?" I watched her face as her chin wobbled a little, her resolve cracking. "I don't believe you. That's fucking bullshit."

Avery gripped her suitcase. "We hadn't figured out an exit for me, but this seems like a good time. It's probably better for me to get out before the news breaks. Maybe you can say you didn't know the truth." She started toward the door again.

"Not so fast. Your real boyfriend can wait. Right now you have some explaining to do to your fake one."

She straightened herself. "You can come up with a story to protect yourself. Tell them Eric hired me without your knowledge. Tell them you had no idea I was an escort. But if I'm here, I won't be able to lie. They'll be able to see the truth."

I took another step toward her. "Just like I see the truth right now? You're lying, babe. There's no one else but me."

"I have to go." She tried to walk out again and I moved to block her. "What I *don't* have to do is see your life ruined and know that I'm responsible for it."

"So which one is it?" I asked, my eyes searching her face. "Are you leaving to go to your real boyfriend's house? Or are you leaving because you think you're going to protect me?"

"I'm going to my real boyfriend's house." The words sounded dead coming from her lips.

"I don't think so." We looked at each other for a beat. "Tell me you don't love me."

She looked as though she was going to start crying again. "I care about you. You've been very kind to me since I've been here. It's been an honor getting to know you."

"Babe. Look at me." I took a step closer. "*Tell me you don't love me.*"

Avery looked at me. "I don't love you," she said. Then she walked around me and out the door.

CHAPTER 21

AVERY

With the money remaining in my wallet, I'd bought five boxes of Kleenex.

And five bottles of wine.

I was in bed, empty bottles on my nightstand and a wad of crumpled tissues spread out all around me. I felt like Lila.

Fucking Lila.

I laughed, and then I started crying again. Laughing reminded me of Chase.

Tell me you don't love me. I'd been so cruel. The look on his face when I'd walked out the door was going to haunt me forever.

But he'd told me the truth: football was the most

important thing to him. And because I loved him, I had to walk away. He couldn't have his football and eat it, too. Or whatever.

I blew my nose loudly.

I'd known this was going to end badly; I just hadn't known it was going to end *this* badly.

I blew my nose again. And opened up another bottle of wine.

~

CHASE

I woke up the next morning and realized something.

I am a fucking idiot.

I told her that football was the most important thing to me. That's because it always had been. I *loved* football. It was my whole life.

But something wasn't adding up. If football was my whole life, why did I feel as though my whole life was decimated this morning?

This got back to the part where I was a fucking idiot. This whole time, I'd been withholding myself from Avery. Keeping one foot out the door. Because of my precious fucking season and my precious fucking reputation. As if I was too good for her.

As if she might be a liability.

But none of that mattered to me right now. Just the fact that she was gone.

Which meant…that I was a fucking idiot.

AVERY

I'd stolen one of Chase's Warriors T-shirts and stuffed it into my suitcase. I smushed it against my face, inhaling his scent, and then roughly put it on.

I missed Chase Layne. I missed his big, meaty hands and his smile. I missed him asking me to make him a snack. I missed snuggling with him and watching our show. I missed him referring to himself in the third person, even though it was seriously annoying sometimes.

I thought about crying some more, but my tear ducts felt dry. *Damn them.* At least I felt a spark of anger—that was better than sobbing.

I decided it was the perfect time to try my sister again.

"Ave?" She surprised me by picking up on the first ring.

"Where are you?" I asked immediately.

"Out-of-state," she said nonchalantly.

My stomach dropped. I hadn't seen any more pictures, but I was taking an educated guess that she was still with Jessica and Pax. She was probably living in their house and making an absolute mess out of it, smoking, sponging off of them and drinking their booze.

A sick part of me hoped that was the truth. They all deserved each other.

"What about you? Have you been keeping busy pretending to be a Boston socialite?" she asked.

"Something like that," I said. "How're you doing for money?"

"I already told you what I needed."

"And I told you that you couldn't blackmail my client." I winced, thinking of Chase. "I can send you some money, if you need it. Just tell me where."

"I'd take you up on your offer, but another lousy thousand dollars isn't going to help me," she sniffed. "I need more than that. I told you."

"For what? Another new pocketbook?"

"No," Lila said icily. "For some self-care that I've been putting off for far too long."

I was getting a Lila headache. "What sort of self-care?" *What the fuck is self-care, anyway?*

"Botox for my lips. They're too thin. And I was thinking I need a breast lift, too."

The silence between us stretched over the phone. "You want *plastic surgery*?" My sister was twenty-five years old, and she was stunning. "What the hell are you talking about?"

"I know you live in a bubble, Ave, and that you have a gorgeous millionaire taking care of you now, but the rest of us aren't living like that." My sister paused dramatically. "*Eighteen*-year-olds have their lips done now. Haven't you watched *Keeping Up with the Kardashians* recently?"

"No. I haven't." *Thank God.*

"Well," Lila continued, "I need to do these things so that I can feel good about myself. I spent my whole life feeling bad about who I am. Don't you want me to be happy? Don't you want me to have proper self-esteem?"

Honestly? I was pretty sure she didn't want to hear my answer at the moment.

I took a deep breath. "Where are you?" I asked again.

She didn't answer me for a minute. "I'm down South," she said, noncommittally.

"Down south where, Lila?"

"In Tennessee."

"With Jessica and Pax?"

"I'm not with The Tooth Fairy," she said.

Even though I'd already known where she was, my stomach still sank like a stone. It still crushed me that she would take this step. That she would betray me so blatantly.

"Why don't you ask Jessica for the money to get your lips plumped up? It looks like the sort of thing she knows all about." An image of Lila and Jessica getting their lips injected side-by-side came to me. "You know what, Lila? I hope you're having fun with her. She seems about your speed."

"Actually, she's kind of bitch," Lila admitted.

"No," I said, in mock surprise. "You don't say."

"If you and Chase give me the money, I won't do what she's asking." Lila sounded earnest, and I knew from a lifetime of experience that meant I was about to be played.

"What's she asking?"

I could picture Lila twisting her hair, calculating how much money she could haul in from all of us. "She wants me to go to the press with your story."

"Lila. The only way Jessica knows about my story is because you got in touch with her and told her. And I'm sure you're trying to get a ton of money out of her, too, while you're busy sponging off them and simultaneously calling *me*, looking to double-dip."

Lila sighed. "If you don't help me, she's the only one I can turn to. You know I don't have anybody else."

I didn't know what to do with my sister. She was the only family I had left, but she made it seriously hard to love her sometimes. "I'll get back to you." At the moment, that was all I could promise.

CHAPTER 22

CHASE

When I was this upset, there was only one thing that could make me feel better. So I took matters into my own hands.

I called Reggie and asked him if he'd meet me to play catch.

I wanted to call Avery as I drove out to the field. But I felt desperate, off-balance. And in my book, that was the opposite of desirable. I couldn't let her see me like this. My face was still red and puffy from…*you know.*

I wouldn't see her until I got my shit together.

I threw the ball repeatedly at Reggie, but my head wasn't in it.

"What's going on?" he asked. "You forget how to throw a football?"

"No. I think I just suck today."

Reggie shook his head. "What are you, hungover?"

"No."

"You stay up too late with that beautiful girlfriend of yours?"

I shrugged, feeling grim.

"Whoa. Seriously, what's your problem?" Reggie looked alarmed. "Is Pax coming back or something?"

I groaned. "Jesus. I hope not."

"So what's up?"

I tossed the football up and caught it, and then I did it again. And again. "Avery's a hooker." I threw Reggie the ball.

Reggie seemed to consider the football for a moment and then lobbed it back to me. "For *real*? They have hookers that look like *that*?" Reggie had been married for over twenty years. He appeared baffled.

I nodded. "For real. Eric hired her so that Jessica and Pax wouldn't make mincemeat out of me in the press and ruin my season. *Our* season."

Reggie motioned for the ball and I threw it to him. "So is she a hooker...or is she your girlfriend?"

"She's a hooker. And she's also my girlfriend." I shrugged. "Maybe my ex-girlfriend."

Reggie scowled at me. "She was your hooker first,

and *then* she was your girlfriend. But *now* she's your ex-girlfriend. Got it."

"That's right. I think it is, anyway."

"You don't seem happy. So what're you going to do about it?"

"I don't know what I'm doing about it," I admitted.

Reggie jogged toward me and tossed me the ball. "But you're doing *something* about it." He seemed pretty sure of himself.

"Definitely." I swallowed hard. "But I'm worried that the press is going to find out about her."

Reggie nodded and caught another pass easily. "Of course they will."

I searched my friend's face. "Does it make me a dick that I'm worried about what's going to happen to my reputation?"

"Naw," Reggie said, ever loyal. "It only makes you a dick if you leave that poor girl because you're worried about it. If you really fell in love with her, and you're man enough to face her past, to me, you're a fucking hero." He grinned. "You're my hero, anyway."

"If I haven't told you lately, Reggie, you always make my day."

Reggie ran out for another long pass. After he caught it, he bowed to me. "You're Chase Layne, for Christ's sake. Nothing to be ashamed of. Show everybody what you got. If you're cool, they'll be cool. Right?"

There was a reason Reggie had been married for over twenty years. He knew when to grease the wheel, and he knew how to love someone after he'd seen the cracks in their pavement.

"Right," I called.

THE NEXT PHONE call I made was to Tennessee. To Pax.

"Huh?" he said when he answered the phone.

"It's Chase. Don't hang up."

"I know who it is. But…seriously?" He went quiet for a second and I heard some muffled moving around.

"What do you want?" he finally asked, his voice low. "I just went out back. If Jess hears me on the phone with you…"

"Oh, trust me—I know. Bitches be crazy," I said.

He laughed and then, remembering who he was talking to, stopped himself. "What do you want?"

"I want to talk to Lila."

"Why?" Pax asked.

"Because I want to take her off your hands. I'll let her blackmail me instead. You won't have to give her the fuck-ton of money I know she's looking for."

He sighed. "I don't think Jess'll let me do that."

"So don't tell her. It's not like she's planning on using her money, anyway. Am I right?"

"She wants me to give Lila a million dollars so she'll do an exclusive interview with us," he admitted. "I told her it's not a good time, with the trade and all…"

"Don't do it," I said. "I'm not even saying that to screw you or to protect myself. I'm serious. It's the man code. Jess is taking so much of my money—trust me, she could afford to pay Lila herself. But she doesn't want to use her money. She wants to use *your* money."

Pax groaned. "You know, it doesn't matter. Even if you give the sister what she wants. Jess knows the truth now about your girl. And trust me, she's not going to let it go."

"You let me worry about that. And dude…"

"What?"

"Get a pre-nup."

Pax grunted. "We never had this conversation."

"Fine. Just put the sister on the phone."

I WAS WORKING my way down the list.

"Elena, it's Chase Layne."

The madam cleared her throat. "Mr. Layne. It's so

nice to hear from you. Is everything okay?" I could hear the strain in her voice. I didn't want to imagine what sort of calls she was used to getting from clients.

"Everything's fine. Avery's great. That's actually what I was going to talk to you about. I'd like to buy out her contract."

"I'm sorry?" Elena asked. She sounded stupefied, as if I'd suddenly slipped into a foreign tongue.

Now it was my turn to clear my throat. "I said, I'd like to buy out Avery's contract."

"Are you *firing* her?"

"It's more like I'm retiring her. She won't be coming back to work for you. Ever."

"I see. Congratulations. Avery is a very good girl. You know she was only doing this because she was trying to take care of that sister of hers."

"I appreciate you keeping this confidential."

"Of course, Mr. Layne," the madam said smoothly. "Please keep me in mind for referrals for your friends. As you know, I have the best girls."

"Will do," I said, relieved that she no longer had the very best girl.

Now I just had to make her mine.

CHAPTER 23

AVERY

Just as I was about to crack open another bottle of wine, Chase sent me a text.

CHASE: Get dressed for dinner. Picking you up in an hour.

AVERY: You don't even know where my apartment is!

CHASE: Chase is wise. He knows all.

Even though he acted like a fuckwad yesterday.

AVERY: I'm not up for dinner.

CHASE: Do you have plans with your real boyfriend?

AVERY: Just stop.

CHASE: I'll be there in an hour. I'll carry you to the restaurant if I have to. So you better get dressed, because you're going out either way.

I sighed and obediently threw on a dress, my emotions see-sawing. I didn't know what to expect. Was he going to say he was sorry? Was he going to tell me it was over, once and for all?

I felt as though I might throw up.

Precisely one hour later, a large SUV pulled up in front of my building.

"Hey," I said, as Chase got out to open the door for me. He looked dashing in a dark suit.

"Hey," he said, softly. His eyes were red and puffy, as if he'd been crying.

I wanted to reach out and pull him to me, but I didn't dare.

We slid into the back of the car in an awkward silence as the driver pulled down the street.

"How have you been?" he asked.

I shrugged in answer, afraid my voice would wobble.

"Am I taking you away from other plans? With you-know-who?" he asked.

I shot him a dirty look. I clearly sucked at lying.

"I didn't think so." Seemingly satisfied, he turned and looked out the window. "We're meeting another couple for dinner."

"Huh?" I asked, surprised. Company was the last thing I wanted right now.

"It's my friend Cole Bryson and his wife. He owns the Rhode Island Thunder. It's a Bruins farm team. Have you ever heard of him?"

I shook my head. "No. Why are we meeting him for dinner?"

"I want you to meet Cole's wife. I thought it would be good for you."

I was immediately suspicious. "Why? Who is she?"

Chase looked straight ahead. "Cole met Jenny when she was on an assignment. She used to work for Elena. At AccommoDating."

I wondered if that was the couple my waitressing friend, Kylie, had told me about. "Did they get married somewhat recently? On an island or something?" I vaguely remembered the story she'd told me.

Chase nodded. "That sounds right. Eric heard about them, and that's how he found Elena. So really, Jenny and Cole are responsible for us meeting. It was like they set us up without actually setting us up."

I groaned. "Is this some sort of escort support group?"

"No," Chase said, his voice stubborn. "I just wanted you to see that there's another couple, living and breathing right here in Boston, who met the same way that we did. And *they're* still together."

"The problem is, Chase, that whoever this Cole Bryson person is, he's not you. *You* are the star quarterback for the Warriors. *You* are in the spotlight, and you have a legacy to protect. No offense to the Rhode Island Thunder, but it's not really the same thing."

Chase shrugged. "It's just dinner. Just listen to what Jenny has to say."

We were meeting them at a restaurant called Ministry, which was a trendy, upscale restaurant filled with long wooden tables and teeming with candles. The hostess delivered us to the table where Cole and Jenny Bryson were waiting. Cole was tall and striking, with black hair, a gorgeous face, and a twinkle in his eye. He had his arm wrapped tightly around his wife. Jenny looked at me with an open expression of approval on her beautiful face. Dirty blonde curls tumbled over her shoulders and her breasts were on prominent, jiggly display beneath a black, curve-hugging dress.

"Oh my God! You must be Avery!" She jumped up and sprang at me, pulling me in for a hug. "Coley told me so much about you! You're with Chase, huh? Chase is my favorite quarterback ever!" She patted the seat next to her and jerked me down. I landed in the seat with a surprised *thump.*

"You want some wine?" Jenny asked me. She emptied the bottle of Chardonnay into my glass without waiting for an answer or for a server to pour it.

"I'm excited to meet you. Cole told me about you two." Jenny held up her glass, beaming at me. "So cheers. To true love. And two men who know not to let it go, no matter what the circumstances." She clinked her glass against mine and took a large gulp.

"Um. Cheers." I took another sip of wine. "Congratulations on your marriage."

Jenny flashed me a dazzling smile. "Thank you. Being married's sort of great." She looked over toward Cole and Chase. Chase was watching us with an intent look on his face. "Maybe you'll get to see for yourself soon. Chase seems like he has an emotional boner for you."

"A what?"

"An emotional boner," Jenny explained. "It's like he's sporting wood on his face. He can't keep his eyes off you."

"Oh. Huh." I didn't know what to say to that. "So, you

know…Elena?" I didn't want to say too much in public. It was a good thing that Ministry was bustling, because Jenny's enthusiasm seemed unbridled.

Jenny nodded, her face serious. "I *do* know Elena. She's the one who set me up with Coley." She tossed her hair over her shoulder in the direction of her husband. "Actually, that's not quite the truth. My best friend, Audrey, was going out with Cole's best friend, James. Well, *going out* with might not be the right term. She was one of Elena's girls, too. Anyway, while she was with James, Cole needed a date. Audrey had Elena send me. The rest is history." She flashed me her huge rock of an engagement ring, fitted snugly next to a diamond-encrusted wedding band. "It was meant to be."

I swallowed more wine, trying to keep up with Jenny's story. "Your friend Audrey… Does she still work for Elena?" The name wasn't familiar, but I certainly hadn't been around the escort service for that long.

Jenny's eyes went wide. "Oh *hell* no." She leaned closer to me and patted my hand. "I wish I had time to tell you the whole story. It was *wild.*"

"I'd love to hear it—maybe some other time?"

"Sounds like a plan." Jenny grinned. "Anyway. The fact that Chase brought you here tonight for a pep talk tells me you're here for the long haul."

I shook my head. I looked briefly at Chase, who was

now engrossed in conversation with Cole. "I wish that was true, but I don't think I can be with Chase. He's too much of a public figure." I swallowed hard. "He's such a good guy. If it comes out about me, it'd ruin him. I don't want to hurt him like that."

Jenny watched me intently. "I understand. But if you have real feelings for him, there's really no getting around it. You can't turn your back on love—you just have to go for it. The rest will work itself out."

Her words made hope surge through me, followed by desolation. Cole and Jenny weren't me and Chase. It was a different situation.

Jenny took another sip of wine, her beautiful, round face contemplative. "Listen, in my experience, there's two types of women who come from our...work background."

She looked around again to make sure no one was listening. "There are the girls who hate themselves because of what they do. *Then* there are the girls who do it because they hate themselves. You don't strike me as a second type, and that's a good thing. The girls who hate themselves are fucked. The first type has a chance, though."

"Oh." My voice came out small. "Hmmm."

Jenny arched a perfectly waxed eyebrow at me. "Right? You see what I'm saying?"

I nodded at her slowly. "Jenny, you're smart. I'm really glad I got to meet you."

She gave me a satisfied grin. "Any time, Avery. I like to do what I can to help. My best advice is to not be afraid of a happy ending. If you grow up the way you and I did—and I don't know how you actually grew up, but I'm guessing—you always think someone's gonna pull the rug out from underneath you. And then you spend your whole life waiting for it to happen." She leaned over and squeezed my hand. "But if Chase is a good guy like I think he is, like Cole is, let yourself have this. Stay on the rug."

I swallowed. "It's hard to trust that another person's going to be there. That they mean it…" I let my voice trail off, feeling a little overcome with emotion.

Jenny nodded, sympathetic. "It's easier to believe the bad stuff. But don't. Give yourself a chance to be happy. At some point, karma's gotta give you a little break, right?"

"I freaking hope so."

Jenny grinned. "I freaking hope so, too."

CHAPTER 24

CHASE

I dropped Avery off at her apartment after dinner. It had killed me to drive away, but I wanted to give her the space she needed to make a decision.

About me.

Eric was sitting on my steps when I got home. "How's it going?" he asked.

"Haven't heard from you in a while," I said, pushing past him and unlocking the door. "Thanks so much for telling my mom about Avery." I wasn't really mad, but I was still having a *WTF* moment about it.

"I did that for your own good," Eric said. He followed me in without asking.

I grunted. "What do you want?"

He shrugged. "I know Avery's not here. I figured you might want some company."

"How did you know?"

"I talked to Reggie." He pushed his designer glasses up on his nose. "And Cole Bryson. I just checked in with Avery, too, to make sure she was okay."

I looked at him sharply. "Was she?"

"She's hanging in there," Eric said.

He went to my wine refrigerator and inspected the bottles, pulling out one that he deemed worthy. He opened it expertly and poured two glasses. "So, I've been thinking…" he said.

"Great. That usually gets me in trouble," I said. I gruffly accepted the wine he offered me.

"You should hold a press conference tomorrow."

"About what?" I asked.

"About Avery. And the fact that she's a prostitute. And the fact that you love her."

"I thought you were worried about her being a liability." I took a large gulp of wine. I still felt guilty about that conversation.

"I'm more worried about what you'd be like to deal with if you had to live without her. Which is also why I had your mother come down. I wanted her approval. We're doing this the right way this time, buddy."

Eric was a pain in the ass, but he knew me better than anyone.

"Back to the press conference. My thinking is, why not?" Eric raised his hands. "You're serious about Avery. The fact that she has a past is just something we have to deal with. And it'll be better coming from you than anyone else. The circle's too wide, now. The sister knows. Reggie knows. Martha knows. Jess and Pax know, too..."

I had some more wine and smiled at him. "This is where Chase Layne surprises and delights his agent."

Eric groaned at my use of the third person. "How are you going to surprise and delight me now?"

"I already scheduled a press conference." I gave him a smug look.

"You scheduled one? *You?*"

I shrugged. "I called my buddy at *WRX* and told him I wanted to talk tomorrow. I told him to bring friends."

Eric nodded at me, impressed. "I like it. But is it okay if I get involved? Just to give it a patina of professionalism?"

"I'd expect nothing less," I said. "You need to earn that commission, buddy."

"I'M SORRY? *What* did you just say?" Wes asked me. He ran his hands through his hair, making it stand up in crazy clumps.

"Avery was a prostitute. I hired her to act like my girlfriend. Then we fell in love."

Wes looked stymied as he paced behind his desk for a minute. He finally stopped. "Why are you telling me this, son?"

I swallowed hard. "Because Jessica and Pax know about it. And they're in talks to do a reality television show. They're going to be doing a ton of press, and I believe that this will be part of what they're talking about. Also, Avery's sister's threatening to go public with it."

West blinked at me. "The fact that Avery was a prostitute. And you hired her."

"Correct."

Coach and I looked at each other for a beat.

"When were you thinking about doing a press conference?"

I shook my head. "Later this morning."

Wes raised his eyebrows at me. "Where the hell's Eric at?"

"He's at the house, plotting." I shrugged. "He's on board with this. He also told me I had to tell you the truth."

Coach slumped down into his seat and sighed. "You think?" He scrubbed his hands over his face. "This is going to be an interesting season."

"It'll be okay." I hoped.

"We're going to stand behind you no matter what. This team has had a great run because of you."

"Thank you. I appreciate that," I said. "I didn't plan this. I'm sorry."

A glimmer of humor sparkled in Wes's eyes. "You can't help who you fall in love with. That's what I told Pamela when I left her for Angie, anyway."

Coach got a divorce last year, but he'd never spoken about it. "How'd that go over?"

Wes grunted. "About as good as the news that your girlfriend's a prostitute is going to go over."

I nodded at him. "Fair enough."

Wes grunted again. "Who said anything about fair?"

I USUALLY ONLY SPOKE TO the press after our regularly scheduled games. I swallowed hard as I adjusted my tie and took one last look in the mirror. *You're doing the right thing, buddy. And, for once, it's for the right reason.*

Her.

Avery was the one. I'd worked hard my whole life to

get where I was, but it wasn't going to mean anything if she wasn't by my side.

Eric met me at the entrance to the conference room. "You okay?" My agent looked a little pale himself, but he seemed to be holding it together. Probably for my sake.

I shrugged. "I'm passable."

Eric looked around. "There's a lot of reporters here."

"Is that supposed to make me feel better?"

"You'll be all right. You're Chase Layne." He clapped me on the shoulder.

"Did you tell Avery about this?" I'd been worried she would try to talk me out of it, so I hadn't called her. I missed her so much it was killing me.

"Don't worry. She'll be watching," Eric said.

"I appreciate it. Everything you've done."

He grinned at me and his eyes sparkled. "Especially setting you up with Avery. I love that I get credit for that, especially because you were giving me so much shit."

"I'm sure I'll be hearing about it from you for the rest of my life."

"You know it," he said as we headed into the room, both of our chests puffed out beneath our best suits.

I took a deep breath to steady my nerves. Every single news outlet was here and the crowd was rowdy, buzzing with excitement. It wasn't every day that Chase

Layne called an emergency press conference. I nodded at Wes and Tim, the owner, already seated up on the stage.

I climbed up on stage and got behind the podium, smoothing my tie. Wishing it was beer o'clock, I cleared my throat. The room settled quickly. "Ladies and gentlemen, members of the press and management, thank you so much for being here this morning." I swallowed hard as dozens of eager faces—faces I'd known for years—watched me expectantly. "You know I don't often call press conferences..."

One of the reporters I knew raised his hand. "Are you announcing your retirement, Chase?"

I nodded at him. "Hey, Pete. I'll be talking about that, too. But if it's okay with you guys, and ladies, I don't want any questions. Maybe at the end, for a few minutes, but that depends on how well you behave." I grinned at them as I felt the curiosity level rise palpably in the room.

"All right," I continued. "So all of you know a lot more about me than you probably should. You know I'm in the process of getting a divorce. You know that I'm now dating a smart, kind, and beautiful young woman. But what you *don't* know is the truth about her past." I paused as what felt like a thousand flashes went off.

"I asked you here today so that I could be the one to

tell you, and to also ask that you continue to respect my team and my own family's privacy during this time. This will be my final season with the NFL. I was going to wait and announce that later, but it's an important piece of why I'm here today. As you all know, football is my life. I've been looking forward to this season my entire career. I intend to play every game to my fullest, and I intend to win as many games as I can for this team. Because I *love* this team. This team is my family."

I swallowed again, bracing myself. "I'm sure you're like me—that your family is the most important thing in the world to you. My team is my family, as well as my mom, my agent, and now my girlfriend, Avery. I will fight for my family, and I will always choose to put them first. I've made some mistakes, but I don't regret any of them. Because without those mistakes, I wouldn't be who I am or where I am today."

I scanned the faces in the crowd. "When my wife told me she was filing for divorce and then subsequently started a relationship with one of my teammates, I panicked. You all know I'm a private guy. I like to keep my personal life out of the spotlight, and I was worried about how these personal issues might impact my teammates and our season. So I took the unorthodox step of hiring someone to pretend to be my girlfriend. And that someone was Avery. I thought that having a new relationship would salvage my public image."

To their credit, no one said a word. They looked largely dumbfounded.

Finding courage in the silence, I continued on. "Avery and I signed a contract, and I agreed to pay her a certain amount of money in exchange for her company. I had second thoughts about what I was doing. I thought it was unethical and probably immoral. I was lying and I was asking someone else to lie, and I was paying her to do that. My attorney has assured me this doesn't rise to the level of criminal activity, as it was a private agreement between two consenting adults. We weren't breaking any laws, but I was lying. To all of you."

I took a sip of water and watched the confused, calculating, disbelieving, and furiously texting members of the audience.

"And I lied to Avery. And to myself."

They erupted into questions and I groaned. Then I saw one of my favorite reporters, Suzanne, with her hand up. I could usually count on her to get to the point.

"Go ahead Suzanne." I shot the rest of them a warning look. "And *only* Suzanne."

"Can you go into more detail about that? About lying to Avery and yourself?" she asked.

"Sure. It's the worst part. It makes me feel sick, and I

deserve that." I looked toward the news cameras, wishing I could look into her eyes. "Avery, if you're watching, I want you to know I realized something. I never told you how I felt about you. I'm an idiot, babe. I love you. I've loved you from the moment I met you. Or maybe since the swan boats...or when you first made me lasagna...or that night with all the shots..."

Eric coughed behind me and I shook my head. "The point is, I never told you that I put you first. That's because I'm a jerk. I was putting *myself* first because I was afraid of what would happen to my career if the truth came out. And it's taken me this long to realize that's not the most important thing. The only thing I care about is you. So this is the public version of my apology. The private one's where I get on my knees and grovel. If you'll let me."

I looked at the press. "The truth is, Avery deserved better than what I gave her. But even if she never forgives me, something good came out of it. I met someone incredible. Someone who's taught me to be a better person."

I looked around. "Okay, that's all I have for today. Are there any questions?"

Everyone started talking at once.

I swallowed hard as question after question was hurled at me. "Are you saying that Avery's a prostitute?"

"Did you pay her for sexual relations, Chase? Isn't that illegal?"

"How does she feel about the whole world knowing the truth about her background?"

I held up my hands to stop them. Eric had told me the questions would be like this and worse, even though I'd had a friendly working relationship with these people for years. "She worked as an escort, which is different from being a prostitute. An escort is legal in the state of Massachusetts, and being a prostitute is not."

Another reporter stood up. "How is management handling this scandal? Their top player, who was slated to be the NFL player of the year, dating an *escort*?"

There was an uproar of more questions being shouted, but Eric stepped forward. "My client's done taking questions. On behalf of my client and Warriors management, we all hope that you can respect Chase and his family's privacy at this time." With that, he hustled me to a side entrance where I could get out of the building unscathed.

Eric clapped me on the back once we slid into the waiting SUV. "You did good, buddy. That was not an easy press conference to hold. You handled that like a champ. I wouldn't expect anything less."

I nodded at him.

"Let's get you home. You have some in-person groveling to do."

We pulled up outside of my house, but Eric didn't follow me out of the car.

"She's waiting for you," he said.

"You got her to come over?" I asked.

"I know you need help sometimes," he said. "And that's what I'm here for."

"Chase Layne loves you, buddy."

"Don't push it."

CHAPTER 25

AVERY

I was pacing around the house. Chase said he loved me. He'd said it out loud, in front of management, in front of reporters, in front of the world. And now it didn't matter if Lila tried to blackmail us, or if Jessica and Pax did an interview about us.

Because it was out in the open.

I thought I might be embarrassed, but I only felt relieved.

And desperate to see him.

My phone buzzed.

Jenny: Nice press conference. I told you he had an emotional boner for you. See you around the rug.

My phone buzzed again.

CHASE: Can you please come to the front door?

I ran to it and threw the door open.

Chase was waiting for me, his brow furrowed.

"Why didn't you just come in?" I asked.

He crossed his enormous arms against his chest. "Because I didn't know if you wanted me to."

"It's *your* house."

"But it's only a home if you're in it." He looked at me pleadingly. "Babe. I'm *so* sorry. This is just step one of my groveling plan. I love you so much. I've been an idiot—"

I threw myself at him, silencing him with a kiss.

Then I pulled back, running my hands down his face and looking into his eyes, which still looked a little puffy. "I'm sorry, too. I love you so much. I was trying to—"

Now it was his turn to silence me with a kiss, his big hands running over my hair and my face, touching me as if he was worried I wasn't real.

Then he pulled back. "So you don't have another boyfriend? A real one?"

I buried myself in his chest and he wrapped his

massive arms around me. "There's nobody but you, babe. There's never been anybody but you."

CHASE

We spent the next several weeks making up, i.e., kissing, looking at each other with googly eyes and having sexual relations whenever I wasn't at practice. I loved the master bedroom at the new house. It had floor-to-ceiling windows and excellent lighting, all the better to see Avery without her clothes on.

The bedroom was great, but I wanted her in every room of the house. It was my favorite new hobby.

We were on my bed. She'd put her clothes back on and I wasn't too pleased about it. "I need you again," I said, trailing my fingers down her shirt.

Avery laughed. "You're nuts."

"I'm nuts about *you*. Speaking of my nuts…"

She laughed again and swatted me. "What about them?"

I leaned down and looked at her intently. "We still haven't christened the dining room. Don't you think it's time we did something about that?"

"You're determined to do it in every room of this

house, aren't you?" She grinned up at me and my cock rose to attention, as if it were saluting her.

"Absofuckinglutely. Are you?"

Avery looked at her watch. "You have to go in for your meeting in half an hour. You really think that's enough time to worship my body in the manner to which its become accustomed?"

I grabbed her by the hips, lifted her up and threw her over my shoulder. She squealed. "Plenty of time. You're getting spoiled lately, anyway. I bet I can make you come in five minutes or less." I proceeded to carry her down the stairs.

"What are we betting?" Avery asked me, while she hung upside down.

"Well if I lose, I'll just keep going. Does that sound okay to you, babe?"

She giggled. "I guess I can live with that…"

I smacked her on the ass as we arrived in the dining room. "You *guess* you can live with that? You're definitely getting spoiled." I gently placed her feet on the carpet, and started unbuttoning her plaid shirt. I loved it when she dressed like this: a button-down shirt, a pair of denim cut off shorts, no makeup, and a messy ponytail. She was so beautiful like that, just so normal and down to earth. And then when she got dressed up, she was absolutely stunning.

She was the best of both worlds. On top of that, my dick fit in her so tight, I swear to God—it was like she was made for me.

"You know I don't like to rush you," Avery said, as I took my time unbuttoning her shirt. "But you really do have to get going."

I dropped her shirt to the floor and then put my finger to my lips. "Shh. No more talking. Chase is in charge."

Avery rolled her eyes but she laughed. I undid her shorts and they dropped to the floor. I sucked in a deep breath as I looked at her, and in the middle of the dining room in a white lace bra and matching panties. "Damn, girl. It's a good thing your mine. Otherwise, I'd lock you up in this house and never let you out." I leaned down and kissed her, our tongues tangling as she ran her hands down my chest. "I might do it anyway," I growled.

I stripped her out of everything else and then picked her up and gently sat her on the dining room table. "Lie back." Her eyes widened excitement as she did as I asked. Her legs were dangling off the table and I spread them wide, kneeling before her. I looked at her beautiful body, spread open before me. I looked at my watch. "Four and a half minutes, I said, leaning toward her. "Now, *what* can I do for four-and-a-half minutes?"

I ran my tongue gently of her slit, loving the taste of

her. I was rock hard as she moaned above me. I loved making my girl come. I licked the tender bud of her clitoris and her hips bucked. "Oh baby…" she groaned.

I circled her with my tongue, licking and sucking until she grabbed the back of my head and ground herself against me. "Oh my God, Chase! Holy fuck, baby!"

I took her clitoris in between my teeth and nipped gently, and then sucked her hard. I felt the orgasm ratchet through her, her body shaking uncontrollably under my attention. She cried out and her muscles clenched and shook. I continue to lick and suck her through her orgasm, until she was babbling incoherently. And then I stood up, stripping down as quickly as I could. "Two minutes," I said, checking my watch. "Turn over onto your stomach and put your feet on the ground. Ass in the air, babe."

She stood up and grabbed me first, pulling me in for a deep, wild kiss. I was panting by the time she pulled back. "I love you," I said.

"I love you, too." She smiled up at me and my heart squeezed.

She palmed my cock and I groaned. "Okay-turn over. Now." She followed my orders and I spread her cheeks and traced my finger along her slit to her clitoris again, rubbing it slowly, making sure she was still ready for me. At the same time, she reached around and grabbed my cock, circling it with her fingers and milking it. I grunted and put the head against her, thrusting and luxuriating against her wetness.

"Baby, I need you inside me..." Her tone was pleading.

"Since I already won the bet, we don't really need to do anymore." Still, I notched the head of my cock inside of her.

She pushed her ass back towards me, taking in more of my length. I sucked in a sharp breath. "We can stop if you really want to," she said, teasing me.

I inched myself inside of her, entranced by the feel of her body against mine. "No fucking way." Her body was so tight, her pussy was like a vice-grip on my cock. "Not ever."

Her fingers were still wrapped around the base of my shaft, the pressure making me feel crazy. Finally, I was all the way inside of her. She gave me one final squeeze of her fingers and then put her palms flat on the table.

She tossed her hair over her shoulder and looked back at me. "Fuck me, baby. I want to feel you explode inside of me."

"God, I love it when you're bossy. It makes me want to give you what you want." I put my hands on her hips and start started to thrust into her deeply, my balls slapping against her each time I entered her. She bore down on my cock, increasing the pressure. The tightness and the heat were making me insane. I could hear our bodies slapping together, skin on sweaty skin, Avery moaning and writhing beneath me.

"Jesus Christ Avery, you're so fucking tight..."

I reached underneath her and fingered her clit, and then she was bucking and shaking beneath me again. Our bodies slammed against the table, rattling it.

"Oh my God, Chase! *Chase!*"

All I needed to hear was my name on her lips. I exploded inside her.

The orgasm ripped through me and my vision got blurry. But I held onto Avery's hips and continued to pump into her, more slowly, savoring every second.

One thing was certain as I spent the rest of myself inside her. I loved this girl. She was mine.

Chase Layne was one lucky bastard.

CHAPTER 26

AVERY

"I think I have a second wind," Chase said. "Let's get dressed."

"Do I have to?" I whined. We'd been doing it *again*. This time in the pantry. Chase had said something about christening it, and wanting a snack...he'd also mentioned the word 'multi-tasking'.

That was my man. Three things always on his mind: me, football and food.

But I knew now that I came first.

"Would you do it for Chase?"

I laughed. "I'd do anything for Chase." Warm happiness erupted in my chest after I said it, because it was true and it felt good.

"Okay. Get dressed."

We left the house and he headed in the direction of the park. Then we walked through it, past Newbury Street onto Boylston. "Are we going out to eat?"

This is Chase—of course we're going out to eat.

"No. We're going shopping."

"Do you have a store in mind?" I asked.

"I do." He said nothing further until we stopped outside of Shreve, Crump & Low.

I looked in the window and wrinkled my nose. "Are you buying a crystal swan?" I asked.

He just stood there, looking at the window and gripping my hand. "Only if you want to buy a crystal swan."

I shot him a funny look. "I think that's a little fancy for me. With my luck, I'd break its neck." I peered at the swan. "I might even do it on purpose."

"Let's go inside." He didn't wait for me to answer. He dragged me straight to the case that held the engagement rings.

"Babe? What're you doing?"

"I'm ring shopping." He examined the rows of sparkling, elegant diamonds in different settings. "Is there one you like?" He pointed to a rectangular cut diamond with a slim, elegant diamond band. "I think that one's beautiful."

"Of course that one's beautiful," I said. "They're all beautiful."

He searched my face. "Is there one you like better than the others?"

I shrugged. I was afraid my voice would wobble if I attempted to speak.

"You like the one that I picked out?" His voice was very gentle.

I nodded.

A sales person came over, recognizing us instantly. He beamed at us. "You see something you like, Mr. Layne?" His voice was eager, but tasteful. This was Shreve, Crump & Low after all. They sold crystal swans with a straight face.

"Yes I do. We'll take it to go."

Chase worked his magic, having the ring sized on the spot. We were quiet as we waited. My mind was racing and I felt as though I was too nervous to talk. After he'd paid, he put the box in his pocket and held my hand, leading me back toward the park. I still didn't say anything—I was worried if I opened my mouth, I'd just start bawling.

"Speaking of swans..." Chase stopped in front of the swan boats. It was late afternoon and they were closed. He looked at his watch and laughed. "I messed up. We can't go for a ride, babe."

"S'okay." My voice was gravelly.

He patted his pocket. "I want to give you this ring

right now. But I'm going to wait. Until things are finalized with Jess and you and I have some time to settle in. Because I want to do this the right way. But I *also* want you to know what my intentions are."

He squeezed my hands. "They are to love, honor and protect you for the rest of your life."

I felt that nervous little bird of hope in my chest glow. It was a phoenix now, a symbol of rebirth, rising from the ashes of my past.

I blinked back tears.

"Does that sound okay to you?" he asked, his blue eyes searching mine.

"It's more than okay." My voice sounded stronger. "It sounds perfect."

He held out his arms and motioned to me. "Come to Chase, babe." And then he wrapped me in a massive hug, making me feel safe and protected. "I love you."

I smiled against his chest. "I love you, too."

We got back to the house and he swooped me into his arms, carrying me up the stairs and putting me on the bed.

He smiled at me. "Are you in the mood? How much do you think you can take?"

"I can go all night, baby," I said.

He snuggled down next to me, happily grabbed the

remote control, and scrolled through the channels until he found HBO.

Then I sighed contentedly as the new season of *Game of Thrones* started, and I held on to the man I loved for dear life.

CHASE

"What do you mean, you booked another trip to Disney? You just took the boys last month!"

I sighed as my mother explained patiently that her grandchildren had made her promise to take them back to see something called The Electric Light Parade. It involved an octopus and took place outside at night. Or something. I stopped listening.

"Fine," I said, cutting her off. I knew she just really wanted to go again. "Just work it out with Ave."

"I will, honey. See you this weekend for family dinner! Reggie and his wife are coming, right?"

"Right. And Cole and Jenny."

"Looking forward to it!" Martha sounded positively gleeful. She'd been on cloud nine ever since Avery and I had gotten married and had kids. She said grandkids were her happy ending.

Speaking of the kids, I heard a crash from the living room. "Watch out!" one of the boys yelled. I heard another crash.

"Did you guys knock over the crystal swan again? Knock it off! That has sentimental value!" I hollered.

"I kind of hope they knock it over," Avery said, coming up and wrapping her arms around me from behind. "Since you bought it for me as an April Fool's joke."

"Babe. I watched you pine for it. It was the least I could do."

Our oldest son, Finn, whizzed by us wielding a Nerf gun. "Onward, soldiers!" he cried. His two younger brothers, Brodie and little Eric, followed him. There were more crashes.

"That swan's not gonna make it," I said.

"Probably not." Avery leaned up and kissed me.

"Mom! Can we have lunch?" Brodie cried, interrupting us. "I'm *starving*!"

I rubbed my stomach and looked at my wife hopefully. "Chase's kind of hungry, too."

She laughed and rolled her eyes. "I know—because you're *always* hungry. You're all always hungry!" She headed back to the kitchen. She spent a *lot* of time in the kitchen. Good thing she seemed to like it.

Things had worked out better than I could have ever asked for. We hadn't won that last super bowl title, but I did get Player of the Year. Which was a nice touch. Since I'd retired from the NFL, I was now a consultant for *WRX*. I got to go to all the Warriors games and then they paid me to dissect them on TV. It was a pretty sweet gig. I never had to miss my kids' practices. I got to coach their Little League teams. And I got to spend all the time I wanted with Ave.

She made me lunch every day. And breakfast, and dinner. God I loved that woman.

Jessica and Pax had gotten married and had, remarkably, stayed that way. Probably because Pax had smartened up and insisted on a pre-nup. Their series got cancelled after one season. They'd been on the reality-series juggernaut ever since, appearing on such gems as *Survivor: The Celebrity Edition*, *The Amazing Race*, and several celebrity cooking competitions. They were fierce competitors. The other contestants often seemed afraid of Jessica, which was smart.

Lila was still living in Boston. Avery had made peace with her, but Avery always seemed to make the best of everything. I still wasn't happy with Lila. But after she'd successfully completed a rehab program, we'd bought her an apartment. And a car. And paid for her to go back to school. And yet, she still managed to be pissy about it. She wanted a Lexus, but I'd bought her a Honda. But that was as close as I'd gotten to justice.

So far.

Eric was thrilled that we'd named one of the boys after him. He flew up from California all the time, happy to play the doting uncle.

He was still single. He told me that he was considering going the escort route.

I smelled something yummy coming from the kitchen, so I headed in. Avery had plates out and she was filling them with enchiladas and rice.

"Babe. You are seriously the best thing that ever happened to Chase Layne." I grabbed a plate and then reached for the bowl of shredded cheese.

"You can't have that." She slapped my hand.

"Why not?" I asked, crestfallen.

"Because it's *nacho* cheese." She said, snorting with laughter. "Get it? It's a *joke*! 'Nacho' cheese. 'Not your' cheese. Hey, why aren't you laughing?"

"Wow. Just…wow." I shook my head. "You tell seriously bad jokes."

She kept giggling. "At least I don't talk about myself in the third person."

"They warned you—they *said* this was for better or for worse. This is what they meant."

"I'll take it." Avery was still laughing. It was good that she at least amused herself.

We heard another crash and I ignored it, stuffing some enchilada in my mouth. *Oh my God, it was so good.* "I will, too babe. I will too."

The Escort Collection

Escorting the Player

Escorting the Billionaire

Escorting the Groom

Escorting the Actress

❧

My Super-Hot Fake Wedding Date

❧

Silicon Valley Billionaires

❧

The Liberty Series

❧

The Bad Judgment Series

USA Today Bestselling Author Leigh James is currently sitting on a white-sand beach, nursing a Mojito, dreaming up her next billionaire.

Get ready, he's going to be a HOT one!

Full disclosure: Leigh is actually freezing her butt off in New Hampshire, driving her kids to baseball practice and going grocery shopping because her three boys eat non-stop. But she promises that billionaire is REALLY going to be something!

Visit her website at www.leighjamesauthor.com to learn more. Thanks for reading!

Printed in Great Britain
by Amazon